OMAR T
IN
UMBRIA
ITALY

Enjoy!

Deamer

DEAMER DUNN

About the Omar T Series:

In the tradition of a light-hearted contemporary mystery novel, enter the son of a restaurateur and an artist, Mr. Omar T Black. He is a jack-of-all-trades, master-of-none, with passions for women, food, adult beverages, art, and adventure. Part travel book, part mystery, part literary reference, these stories are fun and culturally descriptive. Chef Omar enlightens readers to local cuisine with detailed descriptions and recipes. Art and literature aficionado Omar is drawn to the mysteries of creativity and thought. Omar T, the man, falls in love, and/or lust, rather easily. All Omar T novels carry a guarantee of lifting your spirits as well as feeding your appetite for good food and great living! These Mystery "Lite" stories, concentrate on something intriguing, rather than violence. Readers are Omar's canvas as he takes us along on his Umbrian adventures. Chapters are organized around each Umbria hilltown that is featured in this book. This allows easy reference for you Umbrian travelers to use this novel also as a guidebook to this special part of Umbria!

ISBN-13: 978-1545128886

ISBN-10: 154512888X

Art by Deamer – Novel Cover, the town of Spello

2nd Addition – Pajaro Street Inc
CREATESPACE and INGRAM SPARK

Editor: Dani Cryer

DEDICATION & ACKNOWLEDGEMENTS

This book is dedicated to the founders and all of the amazing people who have found their way to Terni Italy and the La Romita School of Art. As the cycle of life expands and then contracts, there is no activity that carries a higher torch with this writer than those with the courage and compassion to seek and find themselves in a multi-cultural experience. Bravo to all of you!

I tell readers that Omar is about 50% me. His other half are traits that I often aspire to. I was or never will be as handsome as he, but he is just as unlikely to ever contemplate anything enough or show enough patience, to bring you a story like this. In this novel, we get to know more about Omar's mother who is also approximately half like my mother. Omar's Mimi is more mystical than *mio madre*; my mother is actually too good to be believable enough to be in a fiction novel. Both Omar and his mother are younger than we, though in my humble opinion, we both continue to outdo most of our respective contemporaries. Like her fictional namesake, my mother is a great artist and I have had the pleasure of joining her twice at La Romita School of Art. This book would never have been possible without this amazing sanctuary and all of those who are responsible for helping the school to make its fiftieth anniversary!

I mention a lot of real people who are associated with La Romita, both staff and fellow students. Though I attempt to honor them in my inclusion, all of the accounts of them in this book, like this story, are fictional. A special shout-out to my friend Jim for being the inspiration behind Jimmy and to my dear friends Andrea and LisBeth, whose real life personalities are big enough and inspiring enough to be behind the character of Sabrina. Most of the history and art mentioned is real. See the appendix for details.

Bravo and thank you La Romita! Keep on going for another fifty years and then fifty more years after that!

Chapters

Page 6 Omar's Map of Umbria

7   Chapter 1 The Unveiling

12   Chapter 2 La Romita and frescos

20   Chapter 3 Torigiano, the & Senza Speranza

31   Chapter 4 Cesi

39   Chapter 5 San Gemini

47   Chapter 6 Return to Torgiano Lungarotti

58   Chapter 7 Valle San Martino

64   Chapter 8 Magic at Carsulae

71   Chapter 9 Terni, Catarina, a Ferrari, and Mishma

83   Chapter 10 Orvieto Signorelli & Fra Angelico

90   Chapter 11 Assisi

101   Chapter 12 Capuchin order

104   Chapter 13 Spoleto

117   Chapter 14 Casteldilago & Arrone

126   Chapter 15 Grief and Art

131   Chapter 16 A fateful return to San Gemini

136   Chapter 17 You got your moose

142   Chapter 18 Labro

148   Chapter 19 Stroncone

155   Chapter 20 Spello & Trevi

163   Chapter 21 Todi and a Special Wine

178   Chapter 22 Catarina's Toy

182   Chapter 23 Marmore Falls

189   Chapter 24 Return to Terni, Bartolomeo di Tommaso

195   Chapter 25 Foligno & Montefalco

200   Chapter 26 Scheggiano

208   Chapter 27 Vallo di Nera

214   Chapter 28 Narni

219   Chapter 29 A Deal

223   Chapter 30 A Discovery

234   Chapter 30 Perugia

244   Chapter 31 A Party and a Celebration

Additional Omar T Goodies

250 Omar T in Umbria Glossary
Fiction and Reality (locations, people)
Giotto Controversy

252 **Bartolomeo di Tommaso
(Terni – Chiesa di San Francisco)**

253 Omar T's Umbrian Recipes
Crostini and Bruschetta

254 Fried Squash Blossoms

255 Spaghetti Carbonara

256 Tartufo (Truffle) Risotto

257 Osso Buco

258 Gnocchi alla Norcini

260 Omar T Anecdotes

262 **La Romita School of Art – About**

263 Additional Deamer Novels and Books

268 About the Author

Omar's Map of Umbria

OMAR T in UMBRIA ITALY

Chapter 1 The Unveiling

I think of art itself as an adventure. I suppose that is why I never tire of researching, enjoying or creating it. My mother, Mimi Black, is the real artist of the family. Not only when attacking a canvas, but in how she lives life—my mother's vision of the world is defined by her artist eye. With her upcoming sixtieth birthday, I convinced her to return to the La Romita School of Art. Not only to once again teach a group of aspiring artists, but to also take me along as her assistant. It took a momentous event such as a sixtieth birthday, to get my 'business first' oriented father to allow Ma to sweep me away from my restaurant duties for an entire month. Much to the delight of my non-authoritarian soul, being her assistant was pretty much a title without any responsibility. This freed me to simply enjoy Umbria and to create some art within this special place in the world. If you look on a map of Italy, you will see that Umbria is basically smack dab in the center. Not only north to south. It is the only province in the country to neither border a sea or another country. Though often ignored, compared to neighboring Tuscany and Rome, its history is rich and its beauty unsurpassed. Its hilltowns remain the region's core population centers, as well as framing so well on postcards.

Imagine a sixteenth century building that used to be the

chapel of a monastery. This structure is now the art studio

for La Romita. Yes, it is a romantic setting and it definitely inspires creativity. After the typically fabulous La Romita lunch in the cozy dining structure, we made our way across the gravel courtyard to the chapel/art studio. At lunch, on this sunny late summer day, we enjoyed a bounty of local prosciutto, classic tomato, basil and garlic bruschetta, pesto and pecorino penne pasta and salad, laced with fresh fava beans. Ah, Umbria! In the studio, my mother sat slightly elevated, behind a worktable, overlooking her flock of slightly sheepish art students. We all sat facing her, behind long shared tables. This was our first day in the studio, so we were mostly in a 'getting organized' phase, when the earth began to tremble. The sound of the chapel walls shaking, was particularly unnerving because less than a month before, a major earthquake had leveled several central Italy towns, only a few valleys away. Later, we would discover that what felt like an earthquake, was actually just a fissure in the wall. It started when Jack, the experienced gent of our mostly older women group, accidently backed his chair into the adjacent wall, while getting up to refresh his very gray paint water. Worthy of a structure this age, his chair's minor blemish on the aged plaster wall, soon turned into a crack. This crack eked out a strange squeal and a rumble that got all our attention. I turned my head toward the rear of the studio just in time to see an entire layer of ancient plaster come crashing to the floor. This was enough to disorient us. You could feel a tension spread throughout the room as our self-preservation consciousness kicked in. We all jumped up from our sitting positions, preparing to flee, as we wondered if this collapse of a section of wall would soon lead to the entire structure raining down on us. Some had started for a quick exit; some were frozen, while others of us were peering at the roof and walls, measuring the situation. Just as I was stepping toward those who were making an exit, Jack brought our attention back to the wall with a shriek of "look at this." His words and the fact that no other parts of the chapel seemed affected by this minor structure change, pulled our attention toward Jack and the fractured wall. Silently and gingerly, those of us who hadn't exited, made our way to where Jack was standing and pointing

"It's a fresco," blurted out, Irene, our German born art refugee who joined the group, just to hang out with an old friend. Sure enough, though only partially exposed, it was clear that fate had pulled off a layer of this ancient wall to expose a surprise of a prize. The fear and sobering feeling of a possible earthquake began to be replaced by the excitement of discovery. This new emotion spread through the group like a soft Umbrian cheese on a slice of crusty Italian bread. For me, I had come to Umbria to enjoy some priceless artistic time, as well as do some investigating for my father. What I did not know, was that I would also find myself in another Omar T type of adventure.

LA ROMITA
UMBRIA   "JACK"   Jeamor
                                ARTBZ.BZ

Chapter 2 La Romita and Frescos

For many of us, when we imagine an idyllic setting, somewhere in Italy comes to mind. La Romita sits up on a hillside overlooking the city of Terni. Its remodel into a working art school was artistically done so that it has not lost its timelessness. Instead of the stone structures looking as if they were built into this beautiful setting, they feel like they grew on the hill, like the accompanying cypress and olive trees. Like any great gathering space, entering La Romita's courtyard has a transforming effect. Its décor is simple and honest. There are a variety of flowering plants, which dance around its gravel floor; the cozy metal benches and also the antique, blown glass empty olive oil containers. The fact that others have been gathering in this space for hundreds of years, hangs in the air, such that it garners a certain respect, reverence. It is easy to just get lost, staring at all the years, reflected in the layers and repairs of the building stonework. It also feels natural to have conversations of deep feelings rather than spewing out anything superficial. Its opening to the hillside above and its ancient olive tree grove only adds to its lure. Not only can olive trees live and produce olives for centuries, it is impossible to imagine Mediterranean history without these craggily, feisty bastions of nature. If you are struggling with a piece of artwork or even a haunting memory, a walk through the olive grove is just the thing for giving some perspective. A walk to the high point in the grove is rewarded with a view of the neighboring sheep and rooster leer. I find the way sheep herd against each other very endearing, comforting. There is something very personal about how sheep stare right into your eyes. The way their whole body is so still as those big glossy lobes lock on. It's as if they understand that they are responsible for the clothes on our back as well as how well their meat matches the flavors of Italy—like olive oil, garlic, rosemary, and lush red wine. Ok, I understand that some of you see Bambi and Thumper when you look at certain animals. As a chef, I am trained to see beyond such labels. Did Disney immortalize a lamb figure in animation yet? Can't think of one. Anyway, hopefully you have gotten an inkling of the beauty of La Romita prior to my chef brain getting off track.

Two sisters founded La Romita, resurrecting a building that had been purchased by their great grandparents, a few years after the monks left. It was used for many years as the family's summer home and farm, primarily for olive tree cultivation and olive oil production. Some of the olive trees at La Romita are over 300 years old! Sadly, the time that has slowly aged this special collection of buildings, has also taken the founders away from us. The vision of Enza and Paola lives beyond them with new family generations taking over. For years, Paola, the art historian of the sisters was a powerful driver of the schools' growth and improvements. Enza, whom we had just lost, was the talented artist of the two. Both women's community spirit helped to interweave the school with the local culture. Enza's American husband Ben, who is thankfully still with us, is conveniently an architect. He is, in fact, the designer behind the conversion of La Romita into an art school. Following the dramatic unveiling of the fresco, Ben was able to reassure us that the structure of the chapel was fine. Apparently, the revealing of the fresco was due to its own overbuilt self, shedding some of its weight. Ben laughed as he recalled the conversion of the chapel into its current use. "Looking back, I remember always having an odd feeling about this wall. It's hard to explain, but I often found myself talking to it like it was alive. Now that she has revealed herself, I can confess that I always had such a sense about it. I used to pass it off as just a respect for the age of the structure. As a restorer, I often feel a sense of time and a spiritual presence left behind by all the souls that have been a part of such a structure. So, my talking and feeling a certain organic quality with this wall did not seem that unusual at the time. In retrospect, I now feel that this creation was, in its own way, speaking to me. It was as if it wanted to be rediscovered. Apparently, I didn't listen carefully enough."

In full disclosure, my father had only agreed to my extensive absence to join my mother in Italy, when an investment possibility arose. Royce's restaurant, named after my father, not only employs yours truly and my two siblings, but has also become home to an investment club. Over the years, my father has developed a network of restaurant acquaintances that has come to span the globe. What has started out as just a friendly circle of friends, has turned into a variety of additional ways to make money for my rather business astute papa. While keeping my older brother Jasper nearby, since he is Royce's right hand man. Father often rents my sister and me out to other operations. You would be correct in concluding that we are both valuable assets to lend, as well as expendable. This has led to some additional investment for dad and some adventures for me. It turns out there is a winery investment possibility in the wonderful Umbrian wine village of Torgiano. Thus, in addition to enjoying Umbria and my mother's art teaching, my father had also aligned an investment investigation agenda for me. Visiting Torgiano is always a pleasure. Visiting any winery is rather pleasant, for that matter. So helping out dad on this project sounded like just some additional fun. The format for mother's art class consists of visits to nearby hilltowns each morning, then returning to the studio in the afternoon to paint. Mia madre sometimes gives some technical instruction to the group, but mostly she is just available to work with everyone individually.

I have an additional disclosure. I arrived in Italy, still recovering from a battle with a bug, as in an evil creature polluting my interior. Unfortunately, it was winning the battle long enough that I had ended up with pneumonia. Before arriving in Rome, I had finished my antibiotics and seemed to be ready to rejoin the human race. But I remained in a somewhat weakened state—a little bit off of my usual happy-go-lucky, up for anything, personality. I not only had my mother and Italy's bounty to nurse me back to health, most of my fellow students were also mothers—whose children were all grown and gone from home. Seeing my thinned face, and hearing about my illness seemed to awaken each of their motherly instincts. Therefore, I ended up with a fleet of aging gracefully mothers looking after me. Though I am a man who won't admit to leaving my thirties, I have experienced enough of life's challenges to rather enjoy being spoiled for any reason.

After a dinner of grilled and smoked vegetables, crusted veal cutlets, and spaghetti carbonara and a little studio time, we all retired to our rooms. I shared a room with my mother, in what is known as the tower. The two tower rooms are above the upper hillside section of the chapel/studio. Ma was already drifting off as I opened my laptop and searched, "renaissance frescos." I chose this search because we knew that the building dated back to the sixteenth century. Now understand, upon the unveiling of the mysterious fresco earlier in the day, there was no reason to believe that this fresco was any different from the already exposed frescos and art of the chapel. These works of art were all considered to have been painted by the Capuchin monks of the Monastery, believed to be founded in 1548. There had never been any indication that any of these fellows had ever had their artwork known beyond the walls of La Romita. This, I had remembered from my first visit to this amazing place with my mother, six years earlier. So I did not expect to discover the artist via Google. I was just enjoying some adult play, as well as refreshing some of my art history knowledge from my two years of art studies.

I was reminded that even though he had lived in the 1200's, Giotto is associated as the initiator of the early renaissance. His master and contemporaries were still lost in the flat, decretive style of the Byzantine era. This would continue into the next century. It wasn't until the 1400's that the three dimensional and non-religious themes of the renaissance would begin to be approached again. Later came the high renaissance of Da Vinci, Michelangelo and Raphael, in the late 1400's and early 1500's. I had remembered that Umbria had frescos by the well-known artists of Fra Angelico and Raphael's mentor, Pietro Perugino. Before I could dig any deeper, my eyes began to flutter with the weary of all the travel that was required in getting to this precious part of Italy. I shut my laptop and placed it on the dresser. I was quickly off in dreamland. For me, this is usually a delightful place to be. I believe I was back in the early renaissance, in one of those ridiculous jester like outfits. I was in a room with a painter up on his wooden scaffolding, painting away on a fresco. However, as best I recall, I was paying no attention to him. I seemed to be chasing around his female assistant who was a work of art herself. Not only because of her lush female features, but also due to all of the various colors of paint that were randomly spread on her wonderfully revealing frock…

Chapter 3 Torgiano and the Senza Speranza Winery

For me, day two at La Romita was set aside to begin my investigations for my father. I drove down the hill, past the tennis club, through the endless olive orchards and through a flock of sheep. I then headed to the E45 highway in my silver non-descript, rental transportation that my father had arranged for me. At least this simple transport was the same color as my 1971 Mercedes convertible coupe that I enjoy prancing around the central coast of California in. My destination was the cozy wine town of Torgiano. The fertile north, central Umbrian valleys, which are located around and between the more eastern town of Montefalco, are the heart of the Umbrian wine industry. All of Italy is alive in the fall for harvest and preparing for the winter. Torgiano is easily accessed off of the highway. Dad had arranged this day for my first meeting with the owners of Senza Speranza Winery. Senza Speranza was a struggling enterprise. My father didn't burden me with a lot of the details of his investigations. He just explained that it was a poorly run business with an exceptional location and some wonderful assets. My father knows that he should not expect me to remember a lot of facts and figures, because this is not my strength. Rather, he relies on my feel for people. One thing all my years in the hospitality of restaurants has taught me, is to quickly sense the personality, desires and demands of people. This history, combined with my nature to stay in the moment, has served me well in serving my master, Dad. He also knows that businessmen can spout out all of the facts and figures that they want to me but that this will not influence me. This is because all of that kind of stuff just goes in one ear and out the other. I'm not sure if it is because my mind is incapable of cataloging this type of thing or if it is just too busy looking for the pleasures of life; like wine, women and song. Anyway, for whatever reason, I seem to sense whether I'm listening to bullshit or something important like someone speaking about their true passion. That aside, I had no idea what to expect when I walked through the aged, wooden doors of the Senza Speranza.

I was greeted amicably by one of the siblings, Enrico. He walked me through the entire Torgiano operation. We then sat down and he outlined the other assets of this wine business.

"How familiar are you with the wines of Umbria Omar?"

"Not very, Enrico. Although my palate has always been fond of Italian wines in general, I have only limited experience with the wines and wineries of your region. I am aware that the grape varietals of Umbria are at least fairly similar to the varieties grown throughout central Italy, like Sangiovese in particular. In America, of course, we are flooded with the Sangiovese of Tuscany's Chiantis."

That's right Omar. Sangiovese is also our principle red variety. Like the Chiantis of Tuscany, our reds are also blends. The Umbrian DOC red wines are blends of 50-70% Sangiovese, 15-30% Canaiolo, 10% Trebbiano, and up to 10% of Ciliegiolo and Montepulciano. Within the DOC 160 ha (499 acres) in the nearby hills received a special designation to produce a DOCG red wine. Grapes designated for this wine are further restricted in quantity and minimum alcohol level. They also must be aged at least 3 years prior to release. The Umbrian DOC white wines are blends of 50-70% Trebbiano, 15-35% Grechetto and up to 15% of Malvasia and Verdello. We also produce some varietal Cabernet Sauvignon and Chardonnay wines.

"But enough talk, here comes Catarina with some wines to taste."

Moving with the confidence of a Roman Goddess, Catarina strutted right towards me. You must be Omar, she announced in solid but lovely accented English. I had stood as she had approached. What would be seen as a normal gentlemanly thing to do, somehow with Catarina, this gesture seemed to be more of a command.

She looked me up and down, making a quick evaluation. "You are rather handsome. Are you Italian?"

I smiled, enjoying the complement. "Actually my family tree is rather diverse, including Italian." Catarina raised an eyebrow and let a slight "hmm," slip through her lush lips. I added, "I've been told that I'm kind of a chameleon. Because my appearance seems to pull from my mixed heritage and adjust to a look similar to wherever I am in the world."

Catarina just batted her eyes at this information. You could say that Catarina moved and presented herself like a royal. This was not so unusual within generational wine families. In Italy, these families are royalty. The fact that Senza Speranza was a small, struggling winery of dubious background, was not apparent when looking at Catarina. She placed herself right next to me and turned her cheek so that I could kiss it and then the other side. Aromas of vanilla, lavender and cumin came to mind, as I inhaled the scent of what was clearly an expensive, complex perfume. Now I don't want to give you the wrong impression. Catarina was not all clad in layers of royal robes, nothing conservative like that. Nor was she dressed typically of one working in the winery. When it came to dress, it was clear that Catarina was into emphasizing her female assets. Considering that this was a business meeting, I also determined that Catarina considered that her best female and business assets were in fact the same thing. Her black boots sported a sturdy yet 5" high heel. As perhaps a small concession to the uneven, often damp floors of a winery, her heels were a good inch thick, rather than a flimsy stiletto. Her black skirt, tight to her rather wide hips, was held snug with a wide black belt to her narrower waist. The neutral gray top was constrained by the size of her chest. Her long toned legs were emphasized by her high heels, patterned see through tight black panty hose and that her skirt hung down only as far as mid-thigh. There was nothing wimpy about Catarina, including her eyes, lips, big hair or the size of her chest. It had been a while since I had seen a Sofia Loren movie, but from my memory, Catarina seemed to be physically similar to the iconic Italian movie star— especially her lips, hips and breasts. Suitable to her star status, Catarina also wore stunning jewelry. On this day, she had a three-ring choker of pearls, with pearl earrings that hung with a variety of sparkly things attached. There was also intelligence and strength in her big brown eyes.

If you have read any of my other stories, you would know that I am often weak when it comes to fighting off a woman. Perhaps I am finally getting more mature. My father's warnings about how poorly the winery seemed to be run, seemed to damper the usually automatic Omar T excitement button from screaming yum, yum, yum, I felt an equal amount of apprehension. I sensed that this stunning beauty could also be dangerous.

That being said, I did like being the buyer, albeit, as just the representative of the buyer. I enjoyed the idea of being in a position where this goddess would have the incentive to be persuasive. Where my father is an expert at making money from a position of advantage, my pursuits tend to be more simple and immediate, if you catch my drift.

Before heading back to La Romita, I had decided to go for a walk. Torgiano is a really lovely town. I would include it as being one of the Umbrian towns that I would call very livable. There seemed plenty of services and cafes, while still feeling connected to the regions history, in beauty and timelessness. I turned over in my mind what I had seen and heard from the Senza Speranza family. What should I pass on to dad at this point? I decided to let go of any such serious thoughts, not a difficult thing for me to do, and just enjoy the charm of Torgiano. It has a wonderful blend of the old and new. I made my way into the Cathedral and studied the paintings and frescos. There was no familiarity to our mystery fresco, but looking at the art of Central Italy had taken on a new meaning to me—the power of a mystery. I asked a practitioner how old was the church? She informed me that it was built in the sixteenth century—hmm, same as La Romita. With that synergy dancing through my mind, I stumbled my way to the edge of town. I discovered a stunning pathway lined on both sides by thirty to forty feet of tall, timeless, Italian cypress trees. The pathway leads to a tower that stretches even higher than the lush trees. As I took in the visual of this very spiritual feeling pathway, an old man approached me. He was rather typical of all of the retirees that you will see in the hilltowns of Umbria. They tend to be the region's most visible residents, often spending their days in the public gathering places. Walking slowly but with a quiet confidence, his steady steps were not aided by a cane. I would not call his clothing tattered or new. Rather, they looked like they were purchased a long time ago but were still in good condition. He greeted me with a "ciao." I responded with the same. Then to my surprise, after taking a good look at me, which included him squinting his eyes and loose eyebrows, he asked, "American?"

"Si," I responded. Chuckling at myself for my apparent transparency. He then went on in very good English to tell me that the tower was the *Torre di Guardia*, a defensive tower dating back to the 13th century.

"Back in its day, our villages were all about seeing and protecting the citizens from the enemy." Following this statement, he went on to add, "I guess we still need a good perspective to spot the dangers of our time..."
I chuckled at his profound observation. Not finding an equal insight to add, I turned my attention to this medieval tower's grand arched entry. It was left open on both sides so that you could see through it, to a very old looking, lonesome piccolo building, in which the path ended. I thought that, perhaps, even though we may not need such a towering protection nowadays, every town would surely benefit from such a peaceful, meditative place as this setting located on the edge of Torgiano. We walked the path together in silence. Once under the tower he asked me if I wanted to climb the stairs and view the region from the top.

"That would be wonderful."

The *vecchio* pulled out a key from his woolen jacket and pulled at the very old door. As it ground and stuck on the stone floor, I reached over his shoulder and helped him open it all the way.

"Go ahead, I will wait for you down here. Take your time. I'm in no hurry." Cleary, he was not up for climbing all of the stairs with me. The beauty of Torgiano and its surrounding hills took my breath away. I understood why my father and his investors would place so much of value in being able to own a piece of this patchwork of vineyards and history. I thanked my new friend and headed back to my car. I realized that we had never even exchanged names. How we meet and interact with our fellow humans can sometimes be so random.

I returned to La Romita just in time for dinner, thank goodness. The combination orange and honey glazed pork, saffron potato salad, baked tomatoes and tossed greens were exquisite. A San Francisco Bay resident and a frequent La Romita teacher of her own, Lisa told us a funny story of my mother sketching and later painting the neighbors' sheep. "She kept walking into the herd trying to get them to align themselves into a better composition. I finally had to put down my pencils and just laugh."

Chapter 4 Cesi

Cesi, Umbria   Deamer   ARTB2, B2

The usual routine each morning at the La Romita School of Art, is to load all who choose to venture, into a twenty seat mini bus, and head off for one of Umbria's hilltowns. Before departure, we receive a map and a short explanation of the designation for the day from School director Edmund. All of the years of hanging out in Italy has not only given Edmund the gift of fluent Italian, he has become quite the Umbrian historian. This morning, he took us to the nearby town of Cesi. Where as most hilltowns sit on top of something, Cesi is carved into the side of Mount Torre Maggiore. The small *borgo* retains its late-medieval appearance, within its boundaries and also from afar. It sits among olive groves that are stretched out lengthwise along a narrow contour of the mountain. There are breath taking views of the valley below, the distant mountain peaks and the slightly north hilltown of Sam Gemini. It is a one public bathroom town, an important measure for travelers. As you walk up from the parking area, the little restaurant/market houses the bathroom and also functions as a popular place for the locals to greet and have a quick catch-up on each other's families. One thing I've noticed in these small Italian towns, is that a quick greeting by a fellow resident can turn into an hour discussion. I had a bit of a slow start as I started up the hill to the first of Cesi's two magnificent churches—yes, I think it is a tradition, if not mandatory, for a hilltown to have more churches than public bathrooms. As I started up the sloping main road, I welcomed the first two people that I encountered with a "*buongiorno*!" They did not respond at all. This made me a little self-conscience, but I kept on exploring this adorable town. Cesi is quite small. Given the fact that my lungs were still in recovery mode, I was rather pleased. I'd say that you could walk every street in an hour. Cars do slink their way up and down Cesi, but they are few and far between. The few cars are not intimidating for the streets because they can only be navigated at a slow speed. When I reached a kind of pinnacle, a very enthusiastic resident greeted me. He was a gray tabby cat. His lair was the basin of the town's public water tap. I gave him some of my best meows, which he found encouraging enough to begin one of those kitty rolls—half stretching, half rolling. His expression was a clear, "pet me," so I proceeded to accommodate him. He was very thankful. He went on to perform some rather impressive curls and meows of his own.

CESI, UMBRIA

Feeling more comfortable with Cesi after my greeting from its fury ambassador, I circled up one of the staircases where I came upon a young shorthaired woman helping a quite older woman. Walking for the *vecchia* was quite difficult and labored. I got a couple of good photos of them, framed by a typical narrow street, lined with window flowerpots. I then continued up in another direction, enjoying the nooks and crannies of Cesi and the glimpses of the farm patchwork in the valley far below. When I hit a dead end and retraced my steps, the *vecchia*, old woman, was now on her own just shuffling her feet a little and facing me. She seemed to be trying to walk a bit by herself but had stopped for a break. As I approached her, she looked up at me and we made eye contact. Suddenly an enormous smile lit up her tired and "I have lived long" face. She then bellowed out a beautifully warm "*buongiorno*." The grand spirit of this greeting, from this woman who was probably not far from 100 years old, shot through my inhibitions and wrapped around my heart. She continued to beam at me as I returned her smile and her Italian greeting. I think it felt equally good for both of us to connect, even for a moment, with someone of such a different world.

Many of the workshop participants had pulled out their sketchbooks and gathered around the benches in the courtyard of the Church of S. Michele Arcangelo. This is truly a magical location. It sits on the edge, with a strong but airy wall to protect all from falling off. In the middle is a tree, which has a wooden and stone bench circling its base, for locals and tourists to sit and enjoy the views. Much of our class was spread throughout the courtyard, armed with cameras and sketchbooks. The mix of the timeless architecture, locals and artists and the stunning views was intoxicating. As I made my way into the setting, I enjoyed a "ciao" and a nice smile from a lovely blond local as she and her wiry little white dog passed me by. I pulled out my sketchbook and filled a page with a local enjoying his morning paper against a spectacular backdrop.

Cesi, Umbria   ARTB2.B2   Deamer

As I wrapped up the rough outlines of my sketch, I had a moment where chills spread across my skin. I felt so enamored and privileged to be among a group of artists in such a magical part of the world that my emotions rewarded me with a physical response. A response that is reminiscent of one of my other favorite activities – yes that activity. I laughed to myself, thinking how women seem better at enjoying simple but spectacular moments like this. Where as, all too often, my gender seems to need something loud or physically stimulating to be so aware. My mood and incredible surroundings, made me vow to work harder on the song portion of my pursuit of the preverbal wine, women and song… Well, at least until someone pours me a glass of wine or an attractive woman sends a twinkle in her eye in my direction…

The church was all locked up, so there would be no fresco study on this day. I made my way over to where Sabrina and Jimmy were enjoying the spectacular view, sitting on one of the benches. I knew right away that I wanted to spend as much time as possible with these two. They were already ahead of me; they had almost instantly latched on to each other. A romantic relationship was not in the cards for these two, given that they both were attracted to the same gender. They were meant to be buddies in spirit, and/or in crime. I just hoped, that on occasion, I would be allowed to eat off of their rich plate of friendship. You see, these two are both of the minds that life is meant to be, above all else, enjoyed. You could say that this is a common thread shared by those who find and participate in the joy that is La Romita. On a daily basis, a satisfying life for Sabrina and Jimmy is to generate laughter as often and with as many, as possible. Jimmy is from California, where he left his partner at home—his mate does not like traveling much in general, especially if it involves an airplane. Sabrina, a veteran traveler, currently from Florida, was recently widowed. As I sat myself near them, it was clear that they were already entertaining each other from their position, side-by-side on a bench overlooking the entire valley of Terni. I must have still had a face that was a refection of my grand cheer of the moment, because they both gave me a smile of appreciation. No words were exchanged this time. We just shared the joy and bond that such a rich experience was bestowing upon us. We each turned our attention to the fields below, the distant mountains and the view of the nearby hilltown of San Gemini. I pointed to it and informed my new friends that we were heading there tomorrow.

Mother was particularly exuberant at dinner. The combination of *tartufo* risotto and crusted eggplant, two of my Ma's favorites seemed to enliven her spirits. She told stories of past classes, with other veterans piping in. Edmund, the La Romita director, keep pouring mother more wine, putting gas on the fire. Edmund, as usual always has a humorous take on everything. As adept at finding a solution for any problem and as talented Edmund is at poetry, his greatest art is possibly how he makes any and all in his company laugh. Sometimes his wit is too heady for some, including the often slow to catch on Omar T. Often, those with quicker minds are chuckling away, as us slow ones involuntary become Edmund's straight men. The wine was flowing and the good cheer filled the dining room.

Chapter 5 San Gemini

International Institute for Restoration and Preservation

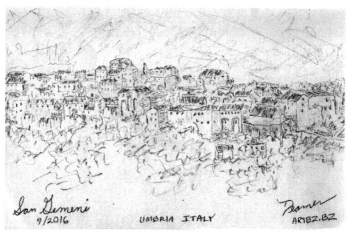

San Gemini is a gem of a small hilltown. The territory of San Gemini dates back to Roman times. Its tall, defensive walls, which grow out of the stone hillside it occupies, helped it survive the Middle Ages and Papal dominance, albeit with its ownership changing hands several times—not an unusual historic phenomenon for Umbrian cities and regions. Its population is around 4500, supported by a variety of shops and several places for food and drink. It's piazza sits right in the middle of San Gemini, which supports a cathedral and a town hall. The rest of the village is pretty much centered along its main pathway, which is Via Roma off in one direction of Piazza San Francisco and Via Casventino going in the other direction.

It turns out that San Gemini is also home to one of the locations of the International Institute for Restoration and Preservation Studies. Thus, the La Romita manager, Edmund, historian Valerio and architect, Ben, accompanied us on our venture for the day. They had a meeting with this organization about our secret unveiled fresco. While they made their way to the offices of the institute, we artists, happily free of any responsibility, were free to do as we so chose.

Once you navigate up the road from the parking area, San Gemini is rather easy and pleasant walking. Not only because it is so quaint, it is relatively flat, thus less demanding—especially for pneumonia-weakened lungs. It is not too crowded, which makes for nice, peaceful wandering. It does have its share of the romantic narrow passageways and beautiful viewpoints. It also has Mariana, whose garden is a magnificent display of greens and floral color. I wandered to her place on my own but later found out that my mother has been dropping by and saying hello for years. Mariana is probably in her 80's but she still gets around enough to keep up the beauty of her garden. I found her sweeping away some debris from the previous nights' somewhat stormy weather. She complained a little but agreed with how the rain made all her plants happy. She beamed when I started my complementary appraisal of the garden. Fortunately, my Italian arranged itself enough with my thoughts so that I could stroke her pride and add some additional joy to her daily chore. After exchanging a couple *ciaos*, I was off to explore more. I did my own minor league investigations of all of the frescos, within the San Gemini churches. None seemed in the style of our revealed fresco, as far as my rather amateur eye could discern. I did however take lots of pictures to compare later. I also came across Jimmy, taking advantage of a patio chair in front of a cute restaurant/bar. I sketched the sketcher against a backdrop of the giant wine press incorporated in the entrance.

The principle town bathroom is housed right in the main piazza, *Piazza di San Francisco*, in a *caffè* with delicious gelato and cappuccino. Like most of these types of cafés, they also have small sandwiches and other sweet treats. Most wonderfully, is its large, umbrella covered, outdoor seating, Like so common in Europe, this *caffè* takes over a chunk of the piazza during operating hours. This not only creates a sanctuary to rest the feet, you also have all the inspiration of the surrounding visuals and interactions. WARNING: if you have never been to Italy, you may find my obsession with their *caffè* and their gelato as over the top. It is not just that they are as good as anywhere in the world in quality, it is also how much their consumption fits in to the lifestyle of the Italian culture, especially in Umbria.

The piazza's Church, *Chiesa di San Francisco*, has a simple exterior with a well-maintained, handsome interior. There are also many classic old buildings in excellent condition, as well as a beautiful peaceful fountain that you can also sit around. Common to many of the hilltown piazzas, San Gemini also has a group of the local men who hang out near the café, day and night. This is all great sketching material and many of us ended up at the café after exploring this charming town. I sketched Salt Lake City resident,

Michelle, as she sketched one of the wonderful facades. Gelato time! A fitting reward for all of that hard walking and sketching. I chose the classic pistachio on this day, accompanied with a bottle of the local spring water, which along with the surrounding agriculture, is a big local employer. The three men La Romita contingent, returned from their meeting with the Institute of Restoration with mixed emotions. Apparently, those they had spoken with had no historic information beyond what was already known about La Romita and its Art. The Institute promised to send over a representative to evaluate the surprise fresco shortly after we returned.

Some of us went back to San Gemini that night for a free concert. A trio consisting of piano, clarinet and bassoon, played in the beautiful old church. Most of us jumped at the chance when we heard that at least two of them were members of the orchestra at La Scala in Milan. We figured anyone who is associated with probably the most famous opera house in the world, would have to be talented. I had mixed feelings about leaving La Romita because we had departed before the person from the institute arrived. I was very curious to hear what they had to say about the fresco.

The trio far exceeded our expectations. To hear and watch the effortless beauty that burst from these three exceptional musicians, in such an incredible setting, was an unforgettable experience. Omar T is not known to spend a lot of time in churches, but when it involves music, you can count me in—a warning, I often refer to myself in the third person, especially when I am engaged in questionable behavior. So, as mentioned, I am not a particularly religious person. That being said, I am amazed at how all music within a church seems so spectacular, even when the regular Joes join into the chorus. Have you noticed that too?

Following a delicious manicotti dinner, I cleaned up the best that I could with my limited attire, for our evening out. Sabrina is one of those women that somehow always looks good. She is the type that keeps it pretty simple, at least when she is several thousand miles away from home. Jimmy, unlike yours truly, always looks sharp. He is the kind of man who never looks like someone dressing out of a suitcase- like yours truly. Jimmy is never overdone, yet is always crisp and stylish. My mother also looked wonderful. Not only in her clothing combination of black, silver and gray, her colorful blown glass necklace by artist Iris Litt, brought out the color in her eyes. As always, Ma wore her smile—that genuine window into her content soul that uplifts everyone who is privileged to be around her. Sitting next to these three made me feel somehow classier.

We were also blessed with a beautiful warm evening, which made our time in the piazza before and after, a delicious treat in people watching. We even had a low moon in the horizon, strategically placed over the church. It was magical, like pretty much everything in Umbria.

Chapter 6 Return to Torgiano, Cantina Lungarotti

Dad had arranged for our whole group to visit the *Cantina* (winery) Lungarotti in Torgiano. I joined them for the winery tour and then headed over to Senza Speranza for my second meeting with Enrico and Catarina. Lungarotti sits nestled in its vineyards at the foot of Torgiano. It is a grand winery, worthy of its importance within Umbria. You might say a model, for what Dad and his investors would like to emulate for Senza Speranza. Before we boarded the bus for Torgiano, I had the chance to talk with Edmund and Ben Over breakfast, I asked about the visit from the International Institute for Restoration and Preservation Studies.

"It was all very interesting," stated Edmund.

"All good," added Ben "They have agreed to take on the project of professionally removing the remaining pieces of the wall, to fully uncover the fresco. As I tried to reassure you all, there are no structural issues with what has come down so far, nor will there be, with what they plan to remove— in architectural terms, it is all cosmetic."

"That is great! Did they have any great illuminations on the fresco itself?" I wondered.

"Like us, they are starting with the assumption that it was created by one of the Capuchin monks living here when it was a monastery," informed Edmund, who then took a bite of the morning breakfast cake, a different one each day, always baked fresh – YUM! Each morning we also have fruit, boxes of cereal, yogurt and boiled eggs to choose from.

"Of course there are a lot of unanswered questions so far," added Ben.

That makes it an adventure, I thought. Seeing the seriousness of Ben's face, I kept such fun thoughts to myself. Seeing his somber face made me realize that as wonderful of a thing that this could be, it was a complicated situation for Ben and the school.

Once I arrived at Senza Speranza, I was disappointed to discover that there was no Catarina to be seen. "No Catarina today?" I asked Enrico rather sheepishly.

"No, my sister has never been very interested in the bookkeeping part of our business."

A woman after my own heart, I thought, wishing that I were wherever she was.

Enrico ushered me to the office, where I spent two hours with their accounting department. Since my ability to absorb anything that resembles a balance sheet is minimal, I was very thankful when they announced they had sent a package of all they would go over with me, to my father. Thus, for the next two hours, I gave them some of my best-raised eyebrows, smiles and general expressions, pretending that I was understanding. Although none of the details stayed in my limited brain, I did mentally note when they seemed a little nervous or dubious in explaining something. It was these reactions that I would later point out to my father. Since I had little desire to understand most of what they were telling me, my eyes tended to roam to the photos on the wall. In particular, I was fascinated by the images of a young Catarina. I felt rather privileged to view the photos of a 'princess,' as a girl, in her youth. Enrico and Catarina's parents were also very handsome and beautiful. They all seemed so happy and prosperous as a family. There were pictures of them together not only throughout Italy, but also in quite a variety of additional spots in the world. I noted that there were no images of their parents getting older. There were pictures of Enrico and Catarina developing into their regal selves, but the parents had mysteriously disappeared from the photos. I remembered that my father had mentioned that the winery was for sale for family reasons. As per usual, I did not recall any details that he may have added. When Enrico reappeared, he mercifully offered a return to the tasting room, to dust off the boredom presented by the bean counters. He poured me a glass of a white blend that they had been working on.

"Wow, Enrico, this is wonderful."

"This is our first attempt at aging a white wine blend in oak barrels."

I took another sip and sucked in some air to help bring out its nuances. "Great texture and I love the cornucopia of flavor Enrico."

"Thank you, Omar, I had to fight the board of directors to make it." He paused a moment before adding. "They still haven't approved its bottling and selling."

This was the perfect lead into what I hoped would clarify the family situation. "Board of directors?" I asked

"Yes, this oversight of the business started as my two uncles, essentially running the business when Catarina and I were teenagers."

"I take it something happened to your parents?"

"Yes."

There was then an awkward pause. I took another sip of wine, giving Enrico time to respond. My palate was starting to be tuned into the wines of Umbria. I could pick out the Trebbiano and Graciano varieties within the wine. I felt there was probably a touch of at least one more varietal. I would guess that they were aged a year in new French oak. I held my observations for later questioning. I wanted to know about his parents.

"My mother died in an accident. And… well… my father was never quite the same. My uncles were both very successful businessmen so they stepped in to save the business from going down. At first this was great. They got things running well again. That allowed both Catarina and I to go off to college in America. I went to UC Davis to study viniculture American style. Catarina went to New York."

"What did Catarina study?"

This question actually cracked up the somber Enrico. "I guess you could say that she studied how to become a beautiful diva that every man would desire."

I smiled back, knowing that she had achieved such status.

"I take it that in the long run, the board situation hasn't worked out so well?"

"That's correct Omar. That is why we are selling."

"What can you tell me about it Enrico?"

"Well, on the one hand, my uncles cared about us, they wanted us to have a successful business. The problem was that over time, the board gained more and more legal control of the business. This wasn't a problem until my uncles both passed away. Turns out, all of the control was passed on to their ten children." He paused again, clearly evaluating what he wanted to tell me. "Ten people of any kind rarely agree on anything Omar, let alone ten from a generation that never had to work hard for all the money that they inherited. Catarina and I were well taken care of for a long time until things started to go poorly. Catarina took advantage of our prosperity in very apparent ways, I have never had any desire to spend much." He stopped again before proceeding. His words and expression showed that he was not certain that he should tell me this, but that he just had to tell somebody. "Basically, I have kept things afloat with my own money because the board hasn't been able to agree on any updates and improvements. I have spent a small fortune on lawyers trying to get control back, but finally I have concluded it is just not possible."

"I'm sorry for all of your challenges Enrico, has it also been difficult on your sister?" I'm not sure why I dared to ask such a question; I guess it was a way to bring beauty back

into this beastly conversation. I was disappointed that
Beauty hadn't joined us in the first place.

Enrico did not miss a beat. "Oh she always looks good and
acts like nothing bothers her, but somewhere inside her, I
think that she is just as disturbed as I am. Though, don't
worry Omar, she is also resolved that we need to sell. Your
father has a great reputation. We feel that his potential
involvement is a very good thing. Catarina is more than a
beauty Omar. She is strong. After all, she was named after
Catherine of Siena."

"Catherine of Siena?" I inquired.

"She and St. Francis of Assisi are our Italian contributions
to sainthood. I won't bore you with all the history of
Catarina. Let me tell you one story that sums up my sister."

I wondered where he could be going with this. There was
nothing that I had seen in Catarina that had me comparing
her with a saint. Nor, I admit, were my thoughts toward her
what most would consider as being 'saintly.'

"When Catherine of Siena was sixteen, her older sister died. Due to the custom of the time, this meant the next single sister in line, Catherine, should marry her sister's widower. Rather than simply obey, she went on a hunger strike until the matter was dropped. I might add that Catherine of Siena never married nor ever became a nun."

"Hmm," I believe I said out loud. Neither marry, nor became a nun. In this I did see the reason for comparison with his sister.

Enrico's confession had made things pretty clear. The management of the estate had become unmanageable; the only way out was to sell the business so that it could again prosper. This was a heavy realization. There was still the possibility that Enrico had a different agenda in telling me this story. I would stay alert. That being said, my instinct told me that he was genuine and what he shared was simply the truth.

I had a nice walk through Torgiano to the spot near the *Torre di Guardia,* where our cozy van/bus would pick us up. Conveniently, there was a nearby *gelatiera*. I found Jack and Sabrina, each enjoying gelato along with some of the locals. I joined them with a half *caffè*, half chocolate. At only one Euro for a piled high piccolo, it turned out to be the best gelato bargain of all of our Umbria excursions. Praise be the simple pleasures! I also enjoyed starting a sketch of them.

On our bus ride back to La Romita, everyone was raving about how much they enjoyed the town of Torgiano, from the lovely San Bartolomeo church, to the wine and olive oil museums. Jimmy showed off a bag full of wines that he purchased at Lungarotti. I had given him a 100 Euro note to buy some wines on my papa's expense account—research dollars well spent. As we circled our way out next to the long line of cypress trees that I had walked through on my first visit, there was the same old man that had let me into the tower. He waved at us as we passed by. Seeing him reminded me that I hadn't questioned Enrico more on what he had meant by his father not ever being right again after they lost his mother. Was he still alive? Institutionalized? I obviously would have to find out more about him.

Once I realized that dinner was lamb shanks braised with red wine & rosemary, Jimmy and I popped the Lungarotti flagship wine, Rubesco Riserva Vigna Monticchio— Umbria's first wine to obtain the distinguished designation of DOCG—an elegant wine with solid structure. Delicious fruit flavors from the Sangiovese, with also some strength of the Canaiolo grapes. We were enjoying it young, considering it can be aged for years and years. None-the-less, its layers came out progressively as we devoured the lamb and simple olive oil and cheese pasta that it was paired with—a real treat. I would write to my father after dinner about how Senza Speranza needs to also create a signature red wine. I didn't mention my vision of my personal wine cellar also being stocked with each vintage of such a special wine—I did drool over the possibility.

Chapter 7 Valle San Martino 57residents 26male 31female

This little hilltown is hidden away from just about

everything. As Edmund, the La Romita manager, put it, "I

really don't know how it survives as a town." As far as

accommodating visitors, Valle San Martino is a one-

bathroom town. This open to the public facility is located

within its one restaurant. Apparently the bathroom is not

always available. Raniero, our bus driver, immediately

checked with the restaurant to see if it would be open. All of

this extra time gave me more time to contemplate the

formidable Catarina. Within my rather simple mind,

thinking about an interesting woman is quite joyous.

The good news was a yes on bathroom availability, but only

from 10am-Noon. Since it was 8:30am, we all tried to take

our mind off of a bathroom break for a while. Since my lungs were still recovering from pneumonia, I tried to get the highest climb out of the way first. I went into the heart of the town and headed up. I kept my mind on Catarina and all her lovely girly parts, rather than my burning pneumonia challenged lungs. I wondered if fate would ever allow me to learn much about the mysteries that surrounded the formable wine princess... San Martino is really small in structures and amounts of people. The streets were very quiet, though I heard a person here and there through their open windows. This town is really vertical. Virtually every house is on top of the one below. I took my time climbing up by stopping often to look and take pictures. I can't imagine ever getting tired of the romance that exudes from these centuries old hilltowns. In general, the living spaces are very small and privacy is at a minimum. The aged stone and old artifacts blend dramatically with the new upgrades and a prevalent show of floral displays. All of the flower window boxes and the delicious pots and plants around doorways fill the stone walkways with magic. Reaching the top of the inhabited part of the town, my eyes were not only rewarded with brilliant views of the surrounding hills and valleys, but I was also greeted by a marvelous stone wall covered with a variety of vines, including grapes and blackberries. The grapes looked like a Riesling variety and I couldn't resist a taste since they looked ripe. Delicious. A barking multi-colored mutt, about the size of a small suitcase, then greeted me. I wondered if his confrontation was for my taking the liberty of munching on the local crop. It took awhile, but he finally calmed to my soothing words.

Now came my chance to enter the small but still formidable church. Though clearly showing signs of aging and neglect, it was still rather impressive for a village of fifty-seven people. I photographed the two frescos, with the plan of comparing them to the newly revealed fresco at La Romita—there was something familiar about them.

It was then that I spotted my next old woman friend. She was slowly making her way toward me, up a slightly sloped road that came from the town's adjacent woods. She was only able to walk about 20 feet before she had to stop and take a little rest. I felt a bond with how my lungs still ached from my climb. She was a tiny woman of about 5'. I continued to look around and take some more pictures. I turned my attention back to her when she was only about 10 feet from me. I greeted her with a smiling, "*buongiorno*!" Her frame straightened up and she began to chat away. I had trouble grasping the meaning of her words so I just smiled and maybe even nodded a little. I walked a little closer, trying to be courteous and hoping that I might be able to understand her better. She continued to talk and I continued not to understand so I decided to take the offensive and try to tell her why I was there. She listened but I could tell that she also had difficulty following my explanation about us being artists and that we had come to see and paint her town. I looked in her bucket and saw that she had eggs. I realized that she had just come from the source and her words now started to make some sense to me. I recognized an expression that we had used as students, while learning Italian years ago when I lived in Europe: *che fai* - 'what are you to do?' I think of this expression kind of like what you might hear from a New Yorker who goes on and on with some of the classic complaints of life in New York. Such rants often finish with, "*ah but whatcha goina do?*" I realized that she was telling me how difficult life was for her as an old woman in San Martino, but "*che fai,*" what are you going to do. I still didn't understand much of what she said in between her utterances of *che fai,* but I was able to nod my head, give her a look of sympathy and add my own *che fai* at appropriate intervals. With a smile and a nod of her head she tightened the grip on her cane and started her way down a rather steep walkway toward her home. I fearfully watched her perilous descent and tried to imagine how many times in her long life that she had gone up and down this pathway? I also wondered if her sixth sense could feel the pain and strain in my chest and that is why she spoke to me of her challenges. Whatever the reason, I was very happy that she had smiled and spoken with me. I then started up the road to the chapel. My lungs burned a little but *che fai*.

At lunch upon our return to La Romita, Edmund was beaming with news about a visit from the institutes' lead restorer—not to mention how delicious was our lunch of sunflower and spinach puff pastry tart. "She walked Ben, Valerio and me through the process and techniques that they used. It was very interesting," beamed Edmund.

I imagined the fun of watching it reveal itself. I had this picture in my head of a severe, tough, no nonsense woman, working away on the wall. I imagined her sternly shooing away us curious painters when we would try to take a peek at her work. At that time, I had no idea how different this woman would turn out to be...

Chapter 8 Magic at Carsulae

There was a time when Carsulae was filled with interesting frescos. What remains are just remains. Carsulae is nestled on a high plateau on Mount Torre Maggiore. It was a rest stop on the Via Flaminia Roman Highway, which pierced through Umbria. There are enough ruins in this preserved park to imagine the Romans, their horses and their belongings, enjoying a night or longer of restful replenishment and entertainment. The small village had a basilica, an amphitheater and a stage theater. With its mountainous backdrop and its stunning views of the valley below, I imagine it was a much appreciated stop. As per our usual routine, we all dispersed, finding our own Shangri-La for the day. I spent an hour sitting in the remains of what was once the grand theater. Little did I know how appropriate this would be, but that is in the next paragraph. What is left now, was the basis of a strong circular foundation system that supported a high arched vaulted ceiling. In addition to the foundation stone work, some of the stone theater seating had also survived the challenges of time. From what remains, you can tell that the theatre was around 60 to 70 feet in diameter. As I stared at the circular remains, I imagined wooden seating, walls and ceiling. Within my mind, the elegant silence of my location was replaced by a scandalous crowd of bellowing Romans, perhaps around one hundred of them. I pictured the interaction between the patrons and the actors. Did they prefer a comedy or a drama? I chuckled a little as a thought occurred to me. As I stared at the remains, I realized that the mortar foundation piers reminded me of a circle of old shoes. I climbed one from its extended toe and settled down and pulled out my sketchbook.[1] This relaxed brain activity also gave me a chance to imagine the life of the Romans and what this scenic spot looked like back then. I also watched my fellow artists navigate the hillside and the ruins. Some were dancing around with their cameras, while others settled down to sketch or paint. I heard some rustling on the horizon to my left. To my delight, soon a shepherd and his flock invaded the meadow below me. They settled into a nice grassy field for some sheep grazing and shepherd resting. The couple of black sheep in a herd of about thirty, added a beautiful contrast to this sublime scene. The shepherd's trusty black and white sheep dog pranced back and forth between the flock and the shady resting place of his master, which was under the shadow of a beautiful, grand oak tree. What a marvelous vision, in this now peaceful preserve, that was once a bustling center for a conquering culture.

As I gathered up my pencils and headed toward the other side of the park, a magical, musical sound of the voices of young women began to fill the air.

---

[1] Recently, a new wooden stage has been added to the remains, allowing some modern day performances.

At first I could not see any of them, though I could tell I was walking toward this clearly scripted dialogue. I was so entrenched in the beauty of these young Italian voices that I didn't even think of the irony of a play being performed today in front of me when I had just left the remains of an ancient theater. As I got closer, figures emerged from behind some bushes and headed toward me. Ten, twenty something Italian women were practicing a play, designed to twist and turn around the ruins of Carsulae. I settled into the grass and wild flowers that were under my feet and began to photograph this most magical sight. Happily, they continued in my direction. Soon, to my great joy, they were dancing and uttering their scripted words all around me. These women were clearly professional. They all projected the words precisely and moved with the grace and fluidity of someone with a confidence only achieved through experience. Whoever had choreographed this play, really had understood a way to have them cover so much space with an eloquence and playfulness. For the most part, they moved in circles, with an occasional soloist moving towards the center. This person would then become a focal point for the others to dance around. Sometimes these soloists would make a sort of announcement, or at least they would become a pillar to dance around. When the troupe paused for a moment to grab a role of yarn for their next scene, a joyful, beautiful girl with long, wavy, dark hair, turned her focus on me. To my astonishment and nervous pleasure, she left the group and approached me. "*Ciao Bello*." Her introduction was not only easily understood, but I smiled at being called beautiful by such a stunning young woman. She started to rattle off some Italian that sounded so lovely that I had trouble concentrating enough to follow her words. It all became clear when she reached into her pocket to reveal a camera of her own. I also understood that she hoped that I would take pictures of them using her camera. "*Certo*," certainly, I responded. She went on to show me the movie option and to encourage me to shoot both movies and photos. "Lola," she introduced herself and reached out a hand to shake mine, after I had responded with my name. I took her hand, gave it a little squeeze and then brought it to my lips for a little kiss. Not only did I receive a sweet little giggle, my gallantry was also rewarded with some applause from the other girls. The troupe continued for probably another 10 to 15 minutes doing a scene where a kind of leader emerged and stepped up on a large stone ruin. Like Caesar addressing the crowd, she exuded words of authority and then grabbed their prop of yarn which had nine leads so the others could each hold on to an end while they all spun around the anointed figure of authority—like a merry-go-around. The woman of the center continued to bark out words of which I'm sure had great meaning. The troupe would add a chorus of musical chants when she paused. The play was clearly a farce, reminiscent of Shakespeare's Midnight Summers' Dream – later they would confirm that it was in fact a version of this iconic work so often performed outside. As they slowed for some direction, my mother called out that is was time to go. I held up the camera and almost as magical as their performance was, the appropriate Italian words flowed from my charmed tongue, "*Mi dispiace, ma, andiamo ora.*" I'm sorry, but, we go now. My new friend jogged over with her effervescent smile and thanked me profusely. Then before I could turn and walk away, the whole troupe broke into applause and cheer, which pulled a deep bow from inside me, led first by my left arm. Since the applause continued, I gave another deep bow, led in the other direction by my right arm. As if I wasn't already living an unbelievable moment, they then, one by one, stepped forward, each giving me a kiss on each cheek of my then flushing face. I was in a musical dream world for the drive back to La Romita. As I retold the story, at that night's dinner, many wondered if my left over pneumonia symptoms or drugs had caused me to imagine it all. If I didn't have several witnesses, I would have agreed with the doubters. Crusty New Yorker Jack, always quick with one-liners, cursed under his breath, " Here, I was thinking how special it was to be approached by a flock of sheep. Then Omar goes and walks right into the middle of a flock of beautiful young women." Jack shook his head back and forth with an appropriate grimace, as all the lassies of our group cracked up. Sabrina later told me that once we were loaded on the bus, she just stared at me in amusement. She said that my blissful expression had resembled those always smiling, brain washed Stepford Wives of the so-named movie. I remember debating on our ride back, whether or not I would ever wash my face again. I believe, I relived each of their gentle, giggling kisses on my cheeks. For some reason, by the next day, my left over symptoms of pneumonia had seemed to have disappeared.

Chapter 9 Terni, Catarina, a Ferrari, and Mishima

Catarina drove up in her red Ferrari. It was now clear what Enrico meant when he said that Catarina, "took advantage of their wealth in very apparent ways." The car not only looked good, Catarina's beauty and accessories looked like they belonged in such a symbol of wealth. In fact, she looked even better than the car—black leather boots that came up to her knees and a marine blue skirt that covered about half of her tan thighs. Her black blouse picked up on the skirt with some matching blue frills that revealed a lot of her prominent chest. Her black leather jacket hung open. The power of the jacket and the skirt/blouse combo was pulled together with an oversized black belt. Catarina had called to let me know that she was coming to break me away from the confines of La Romita. Her heels crunched the courtyard gravel with authority as I led her to the chapel. As we walked past the dining room, the cook's mouths dropped open with one look at Catarina. There was a similar response as we entered the studio—including from my mother. I wonder what it is like to go through life commanding such attention? Was Catarina ever an awkward young woman? Somehow I doubted it. Before she had her woman's figure, I imagine she still found ways to be the center of everyone's consideration. Not only did she look fabulous, she moved like a princess. I'm not sure who seemed more intimidated by Catarina's presence, the men or the women? Sabrina was clearly suppressing a snicker. I took her smile and twinkle in her eye as meaning something like, "you go Omar." Only Jimmy seemed unimpressed, I would say that his expression was one of being amused. He was the only one of us who could compete with Catarina for style and polish. I wondered if his expression were more due to his confidence or his understanding how I was clearly out of my league with this royal beauty. He would notice that I wore the same blazer and pants that I had strung on me for the San Gemini recital. These were the only upscale clothes that I brought along with all of my scraggly artist drapes.

My mother quickly recovered from the shock of the appearance of Catarina. She introduced herself, took Catarina by the arm and walked her down the chapel, introducing her to each of our gang of artistic thieves. I smiled at how my mother, semi retired former co-restaurant owner, could still be such a gracious host.

"And here, starting to reveal itself, is our mysterious fresco."

Catarina made her way around the loose rubble on the floor and took a closer look. She then put into words what my mind hadn't been quite able to come up with. "Whoever made this wasn't happy." She pointed at a male face on the mostly exposed figure. Look at the anguish in his eyes. He seems unhappy with whatever is his situation. I looked closer and concluded that she was right. "And this one," she was pointing at a partially exposed character of someone that appeared to be in the clothing of power. "If he were a cardinal or royal, an ordinary painter wouldn't dare give him such a posture that is so not regal."

"Hmm," was all that I could come up with at the time. I turned my attention toward Catarina's spectacular profile. I not only admired her elegant and powerful Roman nose, I began to appreciate that perhaps there was more behind it than I had been giving credit.

With farewells, we drove off in her Ferrari, down the hill toward the town of Terni. "For all of Terni's mish mash of industry and commercialization, it does have a center. A couple of blocks of *Corso Tacito* and some its connecting roads are closed to traffic. Here we can walk, shop and grab a bite without dodging automobiles and vespas every second. During the day, you will see a collection of families, retirees and their dogs, strolling and sitting around the piazzas and cafes. There is also a lively group of young people and bohemian types that gather in the evening for a little nightlife. I'm particularly fond of the bar Mishima. It not only has some style, but they have live music and other happenings that keep things interesting. In fact, the director of your school, Edmund and his friend Valerio, played here last Friday."

"He did, I mean they did?"

"Yep. It was very eclectic. Some spoken word poetry and some jazzy style music – fun."

"Hmm," I responded. Two gents of hidden talents I thought.

As Catarina effortlessly negotiated the narrow downhill turns in her Ferrari, I took a closer look at this woman whom I had been apparently selling short. Her beauty and flash was always apparent. But there was clearly more to Catarina than what I assumed. She had amazed me twice in less than a half hour. First her quick and interesting appraisal of the exposed fresco and now, she could apparently appreciate eclectic entertainment.

"*Imbecille!*" Catarina's rant at a driver squeezing by us brought me back to the lassie I thought I knew. Funny how easy it is to interpret a word, although with quite a different pronunciation, when it is spoken with a familiar distain.

Parking in an Italian city is usually creative if not downright impossible. No problem for Catarina. She flicked a switch and a garage door opened. One more puff of that unique puff of a Ferrari engine and we were safely parked in the Terni office building of Senza Speranza.

"One reason I like coming to Terni for a drink," stated Catarina. "I don't like leaving the Ferrari just anywhere."

I would think not, I thought. I wiped my somewhat sheepish expression off my face and gave her an Omar T smile. She returned it with a beauty of her own.

"Nice garage," I commented as my eyes danced around all the cases of wine surrounding us.

"Yes, this is our local distribution center. In other words, from this stock our drivers satisfy all of our Umbria accounts."

"I see," I said, as my business hat figuratively landed on my disorganized mind long enough to take it in to report back to my father.

"I will show you around another time," added Catarina. She seemed more in a play with Omar mood, rather than convince Omar to buy the business frame of mind. That was fine by me.

As the Garage door closed behind us, Catarina put her arm firmly around mine and led me down the cobblestone and concrete pathways of Corso Camelio Tacito. She walked with a vigorous pace, much the way she drove her Ferrari I thought—keeping up with her was a challenge, it was also a privilege. Having such a stunning woman walking arm and arm with me was an unbridled boost to my ego. As Catarina pointed out shop after shop and whether they were worthy of her patronage, I soaked in how virtually everyone we passed stared at her and by association, yours truly. We were strolling on Corso Tacito, no autos—a pedestrian friendly section of Terni. After asking if I knew much of Terni and its history and finding out that I didn't, she gave me a bit of a lesson. "I think of Assisi and Saint Francis as Umbria's soul. Perugia gives us our style and connects our past with the modern world. Spoleto and Orvieto are more our heart, and our creativity. I think of Terni as Umbria's backbone. You might say that the rest of Umbria couldn't stand on its own without the structure of Terni. This valley has always been rich in water and resources. People have fought over it for millenniums. Its development as an industrial center grew Umbria's prominence within Italy. It also made it a principle target for the allied bombers in World War II. A great deal of the city was leveled." She paused a moment with this somber thought before adding, "I think of Terni as being Bi-polar."

"Bi-Polar?" I asked.

"In that its personality and history is rather extreme."

"Such as?"

"Terni is rich in natural resources that are now dominated by man's industries. Despite its recognition as a commercial hub, its patron saint is Valentine and his message of love. If you look at a map, the city looks rather planned out, in a kind of circular pattern. But for those who don't know its streets, it seems laid out by a drunken pirate – complete chaos."

TERNI UMBRIA   Deamer ART82,82

Bar Mishima turned out to be not only refreshing in an adult seeking beverage way, it also helped return me to a place of comfort, given the superior status of my lady friend for the evening. Catarina introduced me around before finally leaving me on my own for a bit. Lucky for me I was stationed at the bar, near 'bartenderess' supreme Misha. Since I was born and raised within the family of hospitality, an establishment such as Mishima, where the owners care about making their clientele feel welcome and happy to be there, means a lot to me. In the manner that Misha quipped and filled the room with her inner joy, relaxed me. Great hospitality workers are usually good at some form of self-entertainment. This puts off a vibe that is not only attractive, it also grabs our attention and makes us want some of what they have. Misha was a classic example of this inner art. She wouldn't just pour a drink. She would dress it up like a mother adding the finishing touches to a daughter's outfit. Sometimes she would even bless it. After watching a particularly grand performance I asked for whatever would get the same spectacular treatment. She smiled and informed me that whatever I should order, would get the same personal touch. Misha is very thin. On this night, she wore a tank top that reveled numerous little tattoos. Unlike the massive tattoos that have seemed to become progressively popular, Misha chose to mark up her arms with a variety of little ones, like one inch by one inch each. This choice seemed to complement both her delicate body size and her vivacious personality. Her mostly blond hair was up in an artistic messy manner. In other words, it was shaped in a bun but strategically let loose in a variety of spots. Some of us can have a particular accessory that is dear to us; something that completes us no matter what else we are wearing. For Misha, it is her oversized eyewear. Not only do they suggest that she can see everything that is going on, they also seem to support the strength of her personality. They also help draw anyone, anytime to the focus, joy and play that dances around her petite playful eyes.

No I hadn't forgot about the Goddess I walked in with. That being said, Misha helped give me perspective. Her mannerisms were like a feminine version of myself when I'm at work in a restaurant. Despite all my comments to preferring play over work, when I am at work in a restaurant, I can't help myself but to make work into play as much as possible. Misha, I could only imagine, has always known working hard, yet she too, has found a style of play in everything she does. Catarina, on the other hand, has had a life where she has had more opportunity to play others rather than entertain them with playful hospitality. Just as Misha is a professional at working in a playful manner, Catarina is a professional at playing and toying with us commoners. This much was clear despite my newfound curiosity with what was now also apparent as to the other sides of this woman. I smiled and said a little thank you to myself. I was silently thanking both my parents for raising me in a world of hospitality and privilege. Such that on one hand I could appreciate all that was Misha, as well as being in a situation where I was out on the town with what I had come to consider an Italian princess. I downed my drinks rather quickly. Mostly, I think so that I could enjoy Misha making me another. Also, perhaps, as fortitude so that I could keep up with *principessa dea*.

TERNI, UMBRIA ITALIA   ARTBZ.BZ

It was also a delight to see how well Catarina 'worked the room.' She bounced around with great vigor, kissing both cheeks on person after person. She commanded attention, not only from her dazzling beauty, but also equally with the strength of her personality. It was this moment that I realized how important her persona was to the brand that was Senza Speranza. In fact, I had an even bigger flash of a realization to pass on to my father. Wine, like the restaurant business, is a lot about the show, the atmosphere around your product. Without quality of food or wine, your business will eventually be undermined. Enrico was taking good care of the product. Not only was I impressed with the wines that I tasted, perhaps more importantly, I felt the passion that Enrico had for making even better wines. Though I am not able to understand the bookkeeping end, it was now clear to me that the winery's folly was clearly in its financial and managerial structure. Enrico had already outlined the problem of family board structure. What was now clear to me was that Catarina and Enrico were clearly the greatest assets of Senza Speranza. I now liked and admired them both, albeit, my friendship with Catarina was clouded by the desires of my male hormones. This I did not try to deny to myself. I was also starting to believe that Catarina respected my family and enjoyed my company. She was fun to be around. Whether she was just teasing me with the temptation of attraction, I did not know yet nor did I really care. I am a man of the moment, and at this moment, I was enjoying being around her. In fact, I was loving everything Umbrian, including this beauty. All I wanted was more…

Chapter 10 Orvieto

Orvieto is a magnificent city. Not only is it grand in its beauty and history, it is thriving with modernity as well. It has a vibrant tourist economy, a special niche in the wine industry, as well as a strategic location just off the A1—the highway that connects Rome and Florence. Fortunately, we planned a whole day in Orvieto. There are so many things to love in Orvieto. For instance, the way it sits up on a plateau surrounded by hillsides dotted with farmland and greenery; how on one side, you have a walkway that allows for a stroll to especially enjoy the view; the way it absorbs tourists so well, fueling its economy without overwhelming visitors and locals; its wonderful farmers market filled with quality selections of the regional bounty as well as all its color and interaction; an incredible buffet of shops and restaurants, much beyond what you would expect from a city of its size; its wine, especially, its white blend known throughout the world simply by the town's name; all the outdoor dining, in particular, all the choices surrounding the cathedral and its enormous open piazza, Piazza di Rupublica.

The cathedral of Orvieto, or Duomo, is not only the second largest in all of Italy, its alternating black and white stonework is very dramatic. Pope Nicholas IV laid the cornerstone for the present building in 1290, dedicating it to the Assumption of the Virgin. In the thirteen hundreds, the choir was expanded and two additional chapels were added. After all of my fresco study, I was excited to check out some artwork by some true masters—the elder, Fra Angelico and the younger Luca Signorelli. The Last Judgment (1449–51) of the chapel San Brizio is considered Signorelli's masterpiece. It was a delight to rediscover the humor amongst the blood and gore of the last judgment. In a corner among all of the epic frescos, is a portrait of Signorelli standing next to fellow artist Fra Angelico. Nothing that I saw inside the Duomo made me think of what has been exposed at La Romita. No big surprise there. Though I couldn't put my finger on exactly why, our fresco seemed like it was from an earlier time. I took many photos and enjoyed the grandeur of the interior. Some of the sculpture on the exterior façade is truly magnificent. I stopped and just enjoyed all of the marvelous craftsmanship. I then walked up the Via Lorenzo Maitani until I found a perfect spot to sit on a wall and sketch the grand entry to the cathedral. I had about an hour and a half until I was scheduled to meet up with my mother and some of the other students for lunch. We had already picked out Cantina Foresi, with its alfresco dining facing the SE corner of the Duomo. Mother ordered their minestrone, which was wonderful. I have never had anything but marvelous soups in Umbria. I thought it a good time to have a porchetta sandwich—Umbria's version of fast food. It consists of various slices, from various parts from Umbria pigs. They crisp up the meat and stuff it into a two hand full Italian roll. It was a tasty treat, though in reflection, I felt a little guilty. With the *porchetta* sandwich being the province of Umbria's many food trucks, it somehow felt wrong to be having one in a sit-down restaurant. I kept my embarrassed feelings to myself. Instead, I had great fun telling, all that would listen, my exceptional reverse roll experience. To my delight, Pat, Mary, Lisa and Flora were all present for my declaration. Though I am personally somewhat immune from the embarrassment experienced by taking pictures of a local, I often do it with my little camera in some unnoticeable manner. While I was sketching, I had two encounters with Italians that really made my day. First, there was the twenty something young women with her rather large, professional looking camera. I had noticed that she was taking photos of interesting things as she headed in my direction. She was clearly more of an artist than just a tourist, for she did not settle for the obvious photographs. As she approached me, I could see her delight in the artistic scene that this disheveled sketcher presented, strategically sitting on one of Orvieto's timeless walls. With the size of her camera, she was in no position to try to take pictures incognito. The lovely sound of her Italian asking me if it was ok to take my picture was music to my ears. "Certo," certainly, was my simple response. I tried to continue to act natural but I was beaming inside. When I was almost done with my sketch, a young couple, who appeared to be locals, strolled toward me. Since they were heading toward the Duomo, coming from my rear, they got a real good look of my sketch as they approached. The young woman chirped out a magnificent, "Bello, your drawing is very good!" Her boyfriend added, "Bravo, senior, bravo."

I did a little more work on the shading before floating over to the restaurant where I could boast about my local's experience.

One reason that I was attracted to fellow La Romita participant Sabrina, is her combination of fearless openness and genuine interest in anyone, anywhere. Orvieto has a way to impress all who have the pleasure of visiting, whether it is the grandeur of its rise above the valley and its magnificent cathedral, its food and wine or its many scenic nooks and crannies. Sabrina felt something more. That feeling of familiarity and interest that makes you wonder if you had actually been in a place in a previous life. Being Sabrina, this feeling encouraged her to walk into a local real estate office, where she met Carlo. They chatted away in a mix of English, Italian and Spanish until they understood each other. Carlo introduced her to Patrick, who introduced her to Dawn and just like that, Sabrina had some new friends and a new idea. They swept Sabrina away from the office to look at apartments to rent. Before the tour was complete, Sabrina had changed her flight home and booked a place in Orvieto for two weeks following our time at La Romita. Jimmy, Sabrina's Umbrian sidekick, tagged along enjoying the spontaneity and amusement of it all. As Sabrina told the story on our bus ride back to our current home, she poignantly added, "The recent loss of my husband has given me a new perspective on how life can be short. I feel such a joy at acting on this impulse. This will give me time to continue to work on the influences that your mother has been making on my art, as well as reflecting on my future."

ORVIETO UMBRIA
DUOMO

Deamer ARTBZ.BZ

Chapter 11 Assisi

I think that most, even non-Catholics, are able to muster up an image of Saint Francis—the iconic image of a simple man in a cloak and sandals—the friar who was in harmony with nature and filled with pure love for his fellow human beings. Tourism throughout Umbria is generally pretty light, particularly when compared to Rome or neighboring Tuscany. There is one exception. Assisi and its association with the revered St. Francis, is filled with tour busses and pilgrims 365 days a year. The town, its beautiful location and the cathedral built around the tomb of the legendary saint, are all magnificent enough to draw a crowd. It is the wonderful stories of the life of Francis that take this place to another level. This was my second trip to Assisi, but on my first trip I had gotten so diverted by a quest, that I had never made it to the cathedral (see Omar T Anecdotes in the appendix for that story). Thus, this time, my biggest quest was to take in the cathedral and all of its dedication to Saint Francis. Most of all, I wanted to study the frescos by the twelfth century painter, Giotto (1266–1337), especially the 28 reliefs of the upper chapel. As a student of art, I had studied Giotto and the art of the early renaissance. Though a medieval painter, his art is credited to being the beginning of what would become the renaissance. He was so ahead of his time that over a century would pass before painters such as Masaccio and Fra Angelico, would embrace what Giotto began so long before. I should explain that I spent much of my youth as a professional student—a student who not only loved the search for knowledge, but also the freedom of little responsibility. Alas, such desires seemed to play a role in the fact that I did not collect a degree in college, culinary school or from the art academy.

There are many wonderful churches within Assisi. To name several but not all, Santa Maria Maggiore (St. Mary the Greater), the earliest extant church in Assisi; the Cathedral of San Rufino (St. Rufinus), with a Romanesque façade with three rose windows and a 16th-century interior;

Basilica of Santa Chiara (St. Clare) with its massive lateral buttresses, rose window, and simple Gothic interior, begun in 1257, contains the tomb of the namesake saint and 13th-century frescoes and paintings; Basilica di Santa Maria degli Angeli (St. Mary of the Angels), which houses the Porziuncola; and Chiesa Nuova, built over the presumed parental home of St. Francis Santo Stefano. Then there is the grand cathedral, The Basilica di San Francesco d'Assisi (St. Francis), which towers over all with its length and its height. It is a spiritual center for Catholic monks and all who value the message of the great Saint Francis. The building of the Cathedral began immediately after Francis's canonization in 1228, and was completed in 1253. The Basilica was badly damaged by an earthquake on the 26th of September 1997, during which part of the vault collapsed, killing four people inside the church and carrying with it a fresco by Cimabue. The edifice was closed for two years for restoration.

The amount of art within the Cathedral's walls is staggering. Brother Elias had designed the lower basilica as an enormous crypt with ribbed vaults. It is covered head to toe with frescos, walls and ceilings. Many great masters of the time filled this magnificent cathedral with the stories of the bible and its followers. Among them are Giotto, Cimabue, the maestro of Giotto, and the Sienese painter Pietro Lorenzetti. Above the alter, Giotto's figures show an emotion had not been seen in previous religious art. In the scene of Jesus on the cross, Mary is depicted fainting. Even the angels express their pain at the scene.[2]

Saint Francis's embrace of a simple non-possessive life, living among his fellow men and embracing nature and its animals, was revolutionary within the church. Giotto was as revolutionary in painting as was the gospel of Saint Francis. Giotto, reminiscent to the pious Saint Francis, seemed to prefer painting ordinary men and their daily lives. This was in stark contrast to the highly symbolic and religious painting of the time. There was a beautiful synergy between St. Francis's attention to all living things and Giotto's depiction of everyday people. I recommend to anyone visiting the Basilica, to begin in the lower chapel. First absorb the predominately, flat, mystical, symbolically religious art, within its relatively dark, powerfully religious

[2] I should note that there have been a centuries old argument of whether they were all painted by Giotto and or if he painted them at all. I should also say that this discussion has progressively been going against Giotto. For the sake of my sanity as an author and your attention as a reader, I have chosen to ignore this argument – if you wish, look up Pietro Cavallini and check the Appendix.

walls. The contrast when you climb the stairs to the upper Basilica is palatable. Not only is this church filled with light, the figures of Giotto are also filled with life. Gone is all of the powerful color of the revered, replaced with the earthy colors of the reality of the time. When his frescos were first revealed they were shocking, representing a dramatic break from the Byzantine painting that the public was used to seeing. There was no gold, no fixed images, no symbols, incomprehensible to general public, just recognizable scenes, showing everyday life, which for centuries had been excluded from painting. Giotto, not only fills his paintings with common subjects, he also brought a brand new kind of three-dimensional realism to these everyday people. He tells the story of St. Francis showing what became so endearing to the followers of this man of faith—his humility and love for all. These paintings were so revolutionary that it would take more than a century for his approach to painting to be built upon—a wonderful symmetry to St Francis's message of non-materialism, which also rattled the rich and privileged.

The first seven episodes recount the story of Francis from his conversion up to the approval of the Franciscan Rule; at the center is the main group of panels illustrating the history of the Franciscan order up until the death of Saint Francis. The last seven panels depict the funeral and canonization of the Saint, together with miracles attributed to him after his death. One of the most famous frescoes is "Francis giving his mantle/cloak to a poor man;" the background is a landscape depicted according to an archaic, Byzantine style. "Francis renouncing his worldly goods" is another famous scene; the figures are divided into two clearly recognizable groups: one portraying his father, representing the past, the other portraying Saint Francis with his hand raised towards God, representing the future. Actually, the real revolution here is the two babies in the crowd: they are the first babies painted in medieval art, which are not a portrait of Jesus.

One of the most famous episodes is "Christmas in Greccio," another innovation by Saint Francis, the living nativity scene. He decided to commemorate the birth of Jesus using people in a little village in the Rieti province. The scene is also an extraordinary document; no painter had ever used so much realism. The viewpoint given the spectator was the same viewpoint that is usually reserved to those of priesthood.

St Francis Giving his Mantle to a Poor Man (Assisi)

Francis renouncing his Worldly Goods

Christmas in Greccio (Assisi)

There was something familiar about the figures in Giotto's paintings, something beyond the remembrance from my art history study days. The more I stared at these frescos, the more a particular thought came to my mind. In fact, I looked around at our assembled group and pondered whom I might share this revelation with.

I wouldn't be surprised if you have guessed what my thoughts were about. I'm no expert, but I had been looking at a ship load of frescos ever since the revealing of our La Romita mystery fresco. And yes, all that was exposed thus far was very reminiscent of the Giotto frescos—in my mind, incredibly so. Why I did not expose these ideas with anyone? Was it that it was impossible for the La Romita fresco to be by Giotto? That is, unless he somehow magically returned to earth almost 300 years after he died. You see, it is a known fact that the structures of La Romita date back to the sixteenth century, where as Giotto, lived from to 1266–1337. Regardless of this known fact, I was anxious to return to our studio chapel and compare the images that were filling my camera, with our partially exposed fresco. As our little bus made its way down route E45, I contemplated the possibilities. The best that I could come up with was that the artist of our fresco was a Giotto fan. So much so, that he created a fresco copying Giotto's style. Of course, so much of our fresco was yet to be exposed, but I had this feeling that there was something similar about them.

For better or worse, I accidently erased most of my Assisi photographs that day—an occasional casualty of our digital age. Regardless, many of Giotto's images stayed in my mind.

To finish our visit to the Basilica of San Francisco, Mother and I slipped down to the lower chapel and then down to the crypt. This burial place of St. Francis was found in 1818. His remains had been hidden by Brother Elias to prevent the spread of his relics in medieval Europe. By order of Pope Pius IX, a crypt was built under the lower basilica. It was designed by Pasquale Belli, with precious marble in neo-classical style. Ugo Tarchi redesigned it in bare stone in neo-Romanesque style, between 1925 and 1932. This is especially important once you begin to ponder the inevitable question of the creation of such a monumental, huge cathedral to enshrine such a pious man—at least for this not very religious fella. Feeling the pure devotion expressed toward the memory of this friar, from such a diverse collection of souls, was very moving. There is an undeniable feeling of love encircling the tomb of Saint Francis. This assisted my departure from Assisi with a feeling of respect, instead of distaste toward the irony of the magnitude of the structure—not to mention a new excitement toward the mystery of the La Romita fresco.

ASSISI
UMBRIA
ITALY

Deamer
AØBZ.BZ

OMAR T in UMBRIA ITALY

Chapter 12 Capuchin order

On this lovely fall evening, La Romita director, Edmund and resident historian Valerio, offered a post dinner discussion on the Monastery and La Romita history. Edmund, being vegetarian, was particularly chipper following a dinner of pasta e fagioli zuppa, fingertip sized rings of ditalini pasta with chickpeas. Along with the lentil meatballs and spring greens salad, it was veggie heaven. Master La Romita cook, Egizia, left out the pancetta to keep this treat vegetarian. Such a presentation was a perfect segue, following our visit of Assisi. A monk named, Matteo da Bascio, feeling that the Catholicism he knew at the turn of the sixteenth century was getting too far from the lessons of Saint Francis, founded a group that would become the Capuchin order. To paraphrase Edmund, Matteo sought to return to the primitive way of life of solitude and penance. As his followers grew, the religious authorities began to see them as a threat. This forced Matteo and his small band to go into hiding. In 1528, Mateo and his group were able to obtain permission from Pope Clement the VII to live a simple, hermit life, with a mission to serve the poor. The early movements growth, slowed with dissention and disagreement with its founders and leaders. By the end of the sixteenth century, the movement exploded with growth. In 1618, the Capuchins became an independent order. They became known for their brown, hooded cloaks.

Valerio, local farmer and sometime La Romita assistant and historian, added, "What started as one man's desire for a more simple religious life, blossomed into a movement. As his followers and influence grew, the Capuchins began to clash with the church authorities." I looked over at Sabrina who beamed. It was no secret that she thought Valerio was just about the cutest man she had ever seen. Valerio continued, "It was 1549 when the construction of the La Romita convent was completed and the church was dedicated to the Holy Trinity."

There are some other keynotes of Capuchin and La Romita history that we are aware of." This was Edmund piping in. "For instance, in 1572, the Marquis Alessandro Castelli (at the time considered a saint) died at Romita, assisted by his guardian Father Giovan Battista da Norcia."
Then Valerio, "In 1578, Girolamo da Narni finds refuge at Romita. He was one of the greatest ambassadors and Preachers of the Capuchins. Girolamo of Narni was appointed "Apostolic Preacher" by the Pope and was so

admired for the depth of his teaching and his eloquence, that after him all the apostolic preachers were always Cappuccinos. And yes, the drink was named after the Capuchins, for that particular brown color of the coffee mixing with the cream was reminiscent of the brown of the Cappuccino monk's cloak. Girolamo's sermons, collected in several volumes, are also a significant contribution to the literature of that time."

Edmund continued the tag team presentation. He spoke about the monastery's well, mill and flocks of sheep. How they supplied much of central Italy with blankets when the plague came to Italy in mid-seventeenth century. It is so amazing to visit Europe, Italy in particular, where history is so apparently all around you. I actually got a little bit chocked up; listening to these two men describe the amazing activities that had taken place right where we were sitting. I started to drift off in an Omar T style daydream, imagining the monks looking at our revealed fresco. Did they create it? What did they think about it? What story was this mysterious fresco depicting?

Chapter 13 Spoleto

SPOLETO
UMBRIA
Deamer
ARTBZ.BZ

Perugia and Spoleto are the two cities of Umbria that have a long history of ruling this region—before and after the Romans and Christians came to power. For a short time, Spoleto was home to the entire papacy rule. There are still some medieval buildings standing, but Spoleto always seems to be transitioning. Construction zones throughout Italy seem to find a way to linger. Maybe it's just my imagination, but Italy seems to take the art of idle cranes and methodical progress to another level. To start with, when you have century after century of building on top of layer after layer of different civilizations, out of respect, change must go slow. Over breakfast, owner and La Romita architect Ben, warned us of some of the current trouble spots in Spoleto. I asked him about the challenges of building and remodeling in Italy. "Basically there is a code against building anything but of course they are nowhere in writing, so it is all about patience and making relationships with the code interpreters, then you can get them to interpret in your favor."

Spoleto, with its long history and its desire to also be a modern city is particularly ripe in scaffolding, cranes, and piles of construction materials. On the one hand, it is interesting to be witness to change; on the other hand, manipulating construction zones can be a challenge. That being said, Spoleto is a city that has so much to offer. Its storied history would be enough to explore with grand expectations. The Duomo and its grand piazza, the fortified castle, La Rocca, with its history of dominance and stifling prison; the well preserved outdoor Teatro Romano, which really gives a feel of how Roman life would center around its theaters; Spoleto's postcard signature Roman aqueduct which so dramatically spans from La Rocca to the hillside across the valley are prime examples. Then there is life in todays Spoleto. It is filled with diverse piazzas, restaurants, lookouts and peaceful sanctuaries. Where some hilltowns offer the calm of a kind of simple life, Spoleto is a place with so much to offer. In this city, I can't imagine ever feeling bored.

In Spoleto, the Duomo piazza and the fort overlooking the town offer places of tranquility as well as beauty. Spoleto, more than any other hilltown that we have visited on this trip seems to thrive on blending the modern, with its ancient history. You see an Internet café with modern furniture hidden in a several century old building, restaurants with classic cuisine but abstract paintings on the walls, modern sculptures strategically placed and even contemporary opera in the century old opera house. As a restaurateur I could sense that Spoleto has a whole different life in the evening. It even felt like the city had a hangover in the morning and that it needed time to wake up. My mother and I had a great time visiting a gallery of contemporary painters—a lot of fantasy and abstraction, great fun. I wanted to spend some time with the paintings of Fra' Filippo Lippi in the Duomo—he is also buried there. I remember being fascinated with Lippi in my art school days. He was raised by Carmelite Friars, losing both his parents as a young child. I loved the story of how the friars finally gave into his desire to become a painter since he would spend so much more time adding illustrations to his texts than to studying them. Then there is the story of how Lippi ended up with a son, Fillipino, who would also become a great painter. He became a friar himself and was appointed as a chaplain for a group of nuns just outside of Florence. While there he met Lucrezia Buti whom he persuaded to sit as a model for him. He apparently persuaded a lot more out of her, at one point. To the dismay of the nuns, he coerced her to his home. The story gets even juicier. Later in life, Lippi met a suspicious death. One belief is that the family of Lucezia or some other woman, whom he had also manipulated under suspicious circumstances, may have poisoned him. All of this rather mysterious, don't you think?

Ma and I enjoyed some quality time in the Duomo. I concentrated on Lippi's central apse fresco cycle of Mary:

"The Annunciation scene," "In transit," "The Nativity" and "The bezel with the Crown." As Ma walked the aisles, taking in all the emotional packed paintings there, I meandered over to the Eroli Chapel, which is decorated with frescoes by Pinturicchio, who I was also fond of. This Umbrian painter, Bernardino di Betto, supposedly, gladly adopted his nickname, Pinturicchio, meaning "little painter." Not being very tall myself, I had some extra respect imagining him stretching his paintbrush to the corners of his canvas. In art school, I would often confuse Pinturicchio with his Umbrian contemporary Perugino. Little P was actually a paid assistant to big P at one time and big P was possibly a consultant for little P's work in the Sistine chapel. I have also heard that art historians often argue over whose work was whose. The dispute even extends to work attributed to Perugino's even more famous pupil, Rafael. Clearly, this 'school' of painters had similar styles.

My mother and I wandered out of the Duomo and took a right down a staircase, which led us to a little park with views of eastern Spoleto. What a spectacular setting to discuss the centuries old creations that we had felt such joy in absorbing. We also had a family discussion, confirming how lucky we both felt to be able to enjoy Umbria together.

A group of us had gathered in the outside Bar Primavera in Piazza Mercato for a last gelato and/or cappuccino or glass of wine—this is another spectacular people watching spot. From the pigeon loving fountain, to strolling tourists, and most of all, the local interaction. I always feel that it is such a privilege to witness those things that give you a sense of the community. Sometimes it is just how someone laughs with the bar barista, the greeting of dogs and babies, or something of contrast, such as, the father who arrived on his powerful motorcycle with his delicate little daughter, clad in pink, contently sitting on the passenger seat beside him.

After an exceptional dinner featuring the classic veal shank, Osso Buco, some of us returned to Spoleto for a Sunday evening opera. The opera house is so beautiful itself that I could have been happy just to sit and watch the people interact with each other. According to my rough math, the theater has a capacity of over 1200. About 250 sit at the floor level and then as many as 200 on each of the 5 levels. Ticket prices are according to place. The stage level goes for 40 Euro, then 35E for the first level ext., with the top floor going for 15E. My mother and I checked our money and decided to go conservative and go for the 20 Euro third-floor. Since the floor levels go straight up and encircle the stage, I don't think there is a bad seat in the house. Each balcony level is broken up into compartments of 5 chairs. Three chairs are placed near the balcony while two taller chairs are behind, allowing the people behind to see over those in front. We ended up with just three of us in compartment #18, so we were all able to sit next to the railing. The white walls encircling the interior of the theater are covered with elaborately gilded gold decorations and a brass railing. The compartments and chairs are lined with lush burgundy velvet that matches the enormous curtain that protects the stage. The orchestra is seated in front and just below the patrons on the stage level. I have never been in a space that so gave me the feeling of how things used to be. On this day, even this rather common man from California, felt like royalty, just being in this place of former privilege.

From our higher advantage point, we had a marvelous view of the orchestra, of which I counted 25 musicians and the conductor. Beautiful music, written centuries ago, by Domenico Cimarosa, who was a contemporary of Mozart, filled the elaborate room. The Opera, on the other hand, was a contemporary farce with 6 opera singers and 9 actors. As the enormous curtain revealed the stage, we received our first indication of what we were in for. Bold, primary colored props, set the stage for the whimsical farce we were about to see. The stage also housed three beds and several couches, which were another indication of the type of romp about to unfold. Even if it were a classic opera, we would have had trouble following the Italian singing, but as for following this crazy affair, we were left with our own elaborate guesses. At intermission, Sabrina ran into an English couple who explained the major points, which she passed on to us. We had guessed some of the plot correctly and the roles of the principle 6 opera singers, but as far as the role of the 9 supporting actors, their wild costumes, and their wild dancing and prancing, their roles were open to everyone's own interpretation. We had some good laughs discussing our interpretations and the things that we had noticed during the play, such as Sabrina put it, "all the humping," underneath the strategic large bed coverings.

Second only to the thrill of entering the opera house and feeling its majesty and traditions was watching and mingling with the other patrons after the show. Looking at how the different patrons dressed and watching how the residents of Spoleto greeted and spoke to each other from the sophisticated to the artsy, was an incredible pleasure. What a privilege to be part of their world for even a few hours. I even laughed at myself for actually enjoying the variety of cigarette smoke that swirled around all of us, as the many smokers left the opera building to visit on its grand entry portico. Many visual memories will stay in my mind from this experience, like the beautiful granddaughter in her late 20's, so patiently escorting her very feeble grandfather to the opera. They both were dressed to the nine's, with everything on him, including his ascot, placed perfectly. My eyes quickly left the vision of his struggle for every step and landed on how handsome he still looked and how beautiful was the genuine love and respect that his young descendent showed with every slow step that she took with him. She had a way of making methodical gestures that somehow made his pathway feel regal. It was then that my attention suddenly became singular. The crowd surrounding me turned into an echo as my eyes locked with hers for a moment. Five foot four, soft chest length hair with strands of auburn, hay and silver entwined equally within the texture of gentle wave, bordering on frizzy. Though thin and tight, there was also something soft and comfy about all of her. Her clothes were layered; they hung loosely around her like the drapes. The colors of her drapes were a conservative mix of khaki and earth tones. These matched her lack of makeup, natural. To counter the comfort look of this description was highlights of metallic weaved within the opaque colors, accented with the strains of gold, silver and bronze that danced around her neck and beyond her chest in a thin, elegant, multitude of necklaces. Though she was talking to another couple, there was a moment where our glances were locked. We both did the courteous break of our stare. For me, at least, this felt like going against the current. It felt like I had to use force to pull my eyes from her. On the other hand, giving her my full attention was as easy as floating downstream. Some six feet separated us. With all of the chatter surrounding us, I could only hear bits of tones of her lovely Italian words, but the way her lips opened and closed was mesmerizing to me. I wouldn't call her lips full or thin, a soft but confident in-between. Her skin was neither dark nor pale, also somewhere in the middle. Tried as we may, our eyes kept coming back to each other. Each time, they seemingly lingered a little longer. Just as I felt my body leaning as if to step toward her, a sudden violent force grabbed my body and pulled me away from this mesmerizing beauty. It was Sabrina and Jim; she grabbed my left arm, he enveloped my right. As they pulled me away with explanations that our bus was leaving, their words sounded like gibberish and our movement away from the woman of my attention brought a darkness over my heart. They continued to lead me away from her, despite my resistance and the twisting back and forth of my head, looking for her. When we reached the bus, I had been shaken out of my trance and was then questioning the whole few seconds of experiencing such a powerful connection to a stranger. Was it my imagination? They pushed me into a seat by the window where I looked in the direction where I had been standing. Both Sabrina and Jimmy were talking away about something or another, but I didn't engage them with my eyes or ears, I continued to look for her. If only I could get one more look… As the bus turned from the side of the Opera house to its front, there she stood, now alone and looking right at me… Or was she? As the bus turned away, her figure blended back into the crowd; I kept my stare toward where she had disappeared until the adjacent hundreds of years old, stone building came between us.

I know what you are thinking, How can I be so taken by this woman when I am supposedly enamored with Catarina. Well, as I have mentioned, I have always been leery of Catarina and her intentions with me. That being stated, I must confess to being a constant victim to the syndrome of being attracted to the next shiny thing. Or, perhaps more appropriate in this case, was how real, cuddly and natural this woman appeared—in contrast to the very shiny thing that is Catarina.

Words seem inadequate when it comes to trying to describe that magnetic draw we get to someone who could be special to us. I did my best to pull my eyes away so that she wouldn't be put off by this weird stranger staring at her. But my mind was blank to the rest of the world. All I wanted to do was look at this woman. There wasn't any part of her that dominated my stare, though all parts of her were quite wonderful. It was more her manner. I just felt happy to be near her, to feel the good naturalness she exuded, the manner that she moved and interacted with those she was engaged with. Of course, none of this infatuation mattered. She was apparently meant to only be a teaser, or perhaps a reminder to continue to be leery of Catarina and the power of her beauty and persuasive abilities. Eventually, Jimmy and Sabrina broke me out of my trance. I was able to basically explain the experience, though not very clearly through the fog of my captured mind. As usual, they just laughed at, and with me. I on the other hand, could not shake the image and most of all, the feeling that vision had placed on me. I even woke up in the middle of the night, doused in my own sweat. I had been dreaming of how we had fallen in love and all the fun things that we were doing together when, violently the earth cracked in half. This was, of course, a kind of symmetry to all of central Italy's earthquake activity. I was kind of delirious; as we tend to be in dramatic dreams so once awakened my memory of it was confused. What I do remember, was that the vision of a woman from the Spoleto Opera House, was sucked away from me into a dark hole of the never to be land.

Chapter 14 Casteldilago & Arrone

In the spirit of discretion, I **was not** going to tell you about what happened with Catarina and me after we left Bar Mishima—the night when she took me bar hopping in Terni. But now that I have shared my fascination of this mystery woman at the Opera, I feel I must give you more disclosure. Catarina and I returned to the Senza Speranza building and her parked Ferrari. Before she drove me back up the hill to La Romita, she decided to show me her office and some other much more interesting things. Let's just say that with or without clothes, Catarina is truly a beauty. Turns out that she can be quite creative and energetic as well. I reluctantly share this with you because at this point you do need to know that our relationship did cross to the other side. In fact, it danced around both sides of her desk, as well as on top. Attempting to not give full disclosure but adequately describing the extent of our play, I will only add that her sexy pair of long black stockings found some new uses and they will not be worn again. As we bounced around her office, I remember thinking it was good that we were into the wee hours. There was less chance we were disturbing anyone. Catarina's strength of personality came out in how she vigorously expressed herself vocally. Though I did not attempt to follow her high-pitched Italian, I imagine anyone who was listening, would find himself or herself blushing. On the other hand, I wondered if Saint Valentine, the patron saint of the city of Terni, was keeping an eye on us. As things heated up, I believe I may have even imagined a vision of him floating over us and laughing with apparent joy. I guess he approved.

As I recounted how the Opera mystery woman had so commanded a physical, mental and emotional response from me, this also brought back all of the fun and pleasure that I had with Catarina. The drive from La Romita to our destination for the day was much too short to really contemplate such big thoughts, so I decided to try and let them go and just enjoy our daily agenda. Two hilltowns, just east of Terni, our base city, are only a few miles apart and face each other. We visited both on this morning. They are situated in a green and beautiful, little valley. It is really cool how you get great views of one from the other. It is difficult to get shots of the hilltowns from distant viewpoints when you are traveling by bus with a group, so the combo of Arrone and Casteldilago was a real treat. Casteldilago, "castle by the lake," is now a misnomer because there is no lake any more. It is a cute, tiny town that we spent just enough time in to climb to the top and back down. As you enter town, we were all enamored with the fig trees that grew right out of the ancient wall. I don't think that I've ever seen a fruit tree grow wildly out of something like a wall and still bear fruit. But these did and the figs were delicious. As I got near the top I met Luis, a white haired little dog about 2' long 18" high. He was a little barky at first, he eventually calmed down and enjoyed a bit of a petting. Later, when Sabrina caught up with me, we met Luis's owner who proudly showed off Luis's ability to catch a plastic bone thrown in the air. He also showed us the way to see the high church and gave us a lot of explanations in Italian that we did not understand, though we did enjoy his friendly enthusiasm. Then as we were quickly leaving Casteldilago for Arrone, Casteldilago is a zero public bathroom town, we met Ocherimo. Ocherimo, who spoke

English well, explained that his name means eight
Rhinoceroses, which duly impressed us and gave us all a
good laugh. He is an electrical engineer who had done some
work on the most damaged town in the big earthquake a few
years ago. He was very interesting and we were sorry that
we had to rush off.

Arrone has expanded quite a bit with modern apartment
buildings and villas surrounding the original hilltown. This
makes for quiet a bustle on the main road and a fair amount
of commercial activity for such a small town. The climb to
the top is kind of a workout, but well worth it for the
serenity and the views of Casteldilago and Montefranco to
the east. As I wound my way to the top, I enjoyed a
collection of 3 very old fiats; a 4 door sedan, one of the cute
3 wheel mini pickup trucks and another vehicle that

resembled a mini jeep. These miniature cars are so adorable.
As I neared the top I spotted the only villa so far that
screamed at me and said buy me and make me beautiful
again. It was across on the opposite hillside of Arrone. A
beautiful 3 level stone building missing its windows and in
general state of neglect. But it has beautiful views and is
still only about 100 yards from the main road. I took a
couple of photos so that I could play with this dream house
later. Jimmy and Sabrina had started talking about buying a
house together here in Umbria. Perhaps I could join in on
the fun? Regardless, I wanted to share this possibility with
them.

As I explored this ancient section of Arrone, I made my way
to a vista point where I had a fabulous view of Casteldilago
and the valley between these two cities. From my height,
the trees and farmland below looked small, like I was
looking at a painting. Suddenly an enormous bird lit from a
tree near the river. Even with the distance between us, I
quickly recognized the unforgettable wingspan of a blue
heron. I had once rented a house on the Carmel Valley
River, back home in Monterey California. My girlfriend at
the time and I had the honor of having one of these regal
creatures live across from us, on the other side of the river.

If you have ever had the pleasure of seeing one of these magnificent birds in flight, you would also never forget their amazing strength and grace. Being among what felt like mostly abandoned buildings with no other human in sight, it felt like this animal's show was just for me. Watching the huge wings glide back and forth, as it circled around the miniature landscape below, took my breath away.

Still feeling a high from my heron sighting, I made my way down the hill to the outdoor seating of an adjacent gelateria and restaurant. Several of our group had discovered that this was an exceptional people watching location. I entered a scene of open paint sets and sketchbooks. First, I told Jimmy and Sabrina about the exciting investment possibilities that I had discovered up the hill. Sabrina laughed and showed me what was on her phone. It was an Umbrian real-estate company. She went on to share some of her favorite finds. When my mother joined us, I shared my blue heron story. My spiritually tuned in mother and Buddhist Sabrina, both had additional thoughts to my vision. "The heron is a powerful symbol in nature and the spiritual world." This was my mother speaking. "The sighting of a heron is considered a predecessor of good fortune and tranquility."

I liked the sound of that.

Sabrina added, "The heron is such a powerful symbol because it is at home in three elements: water, earth and air." This suggests that you seek strength from diversity, which will feed confidence in your pursuits."

My mother picked up on Sabrina's interpretation, "the heron's grace and diversity is also a symbol of easy transitions. If you find yourself in liminal spaces, that is, if you find yourself 'in-between' phases, places or people in your life, the heron can give you guidance on how to easily move through those 'in-between' moments of your life."

This was a lot for my limited brain to contemplate. I got myself a second cappuccino while seeking its guidance and spirit. As the others turned their attention back to the market across the street and its offering of artistic inspiration from all of its wonderful local interaction, I worked on what my mind always tries its best to accomplish – making the best out of a situation and grasping onto whatever information supports the best scenario. "Tranquility and good fortune are always good." Repeating their association with my 'sighting' made me smile. I interpreted the easy transitions with the good fortune as meaning that if I should join

Jimmy and Sabrina in investing into a piece of Umbria, that it would work out well. Finally, I latched onto diversity meaning it was appropriate to be enjoying the company of a powerful, princess type of woman while still longing after the tranquility and beauty of another woman. You may find such thoughts as rather opportunist, this I cannot deny, nor do I feel apologetic for it. None-the-less, I felt very happy with my visions: the heron, a naked Catarina and the peace and comfort I felt just being in the presence of the mystery woman.

This inspired me to get a gelato of lemon and pistachio, while the others locked into the scene across the street at the market. I felt too preoccupied with joy to participate other than with my eyes. For a long time an old man sat very still in a chair with the fruits and vegetables on both sides of him. He alone and his interactions with other shoppers were great sketching material. Gradually, we got to know from our safe distance, the market owner and the two young women who worked for her, especially when a baby appeared and everyone got into the role of surrogate mother. Sabrina, being Sabrina, finally went over to see what the store looked like inside and to try to talk to the family. As usual, she wanted to understand the actual family structure and learn more about Arrone for all of our benefit. Another beautiful day with some more quality adventures. Umbria is magical.

I remained in a kind of hypnotic mist for the rest of the day. I do remember our lunch of Pizza with fava bean pesto, black olives & Taleggio cheese, but the rest of the afternoon was kind of a blur. Edmund mentioned at lunch that the folks from the institute had set up a working area around the fresco. Once we adjourned to the studio for our afternoon art session, we could see how they had blocked off the area, making a cave like working area under draped tarps. I kept drifting back to my visions of the mystery woman at the opera and my blue heron sighting. It seemed that I was surrounded by mysteries.

Chapter 15 Grief and Art

As artists we suffer grief on a regular basis as we give birth to artwork that doesn't always work out. Sometimes we are able to take the grief of life and put the power of this emotion into our work. Grief and misfortune can also lead people to art, both as a solace and as a salvation. Grief will probably always be a part of the La Romita experience. La Romita, as an art retreat, was founded 50 years ago and it has seen its share of grief and loss in those who have participated and those who have helped it operate. There is a lovely shrine on the property, which is dedicated to those who have helped La Romita to be so important, to so many of us. Many widows and those suffering from other types of grief have discovered La Romita and Umbria to be places where they can find some peace and inspiration for healing. Our group has several widows and Sabrina's recent loss has made us all think about grief and how it has entered all of our lives. Everyone of our group is old enough that we have all felt the grief of losing people close to us.

Feeling Sabrina's pain, Jimmy piped in with some wisdom. "Grief is a strange egg. It is always around us but most of the time, for most of us, we successfully ignore it. Then it comes up and bites us in the ass and shakes up everything about us. Grief damages us. We can candy coat it all that we want, but it damages our mind, our heart and our soul. All we can do in the short run is try and cloud the damage with the beautiful memories that were so special that we now grieve at the loss of this person or animal. In the long run we have to make some sort of peace with their death and we rebuild ourselves by adding more quality memories. I don't think that the grief goes away. I think it just finds a healthier place to reside inside of us while we build new good memories."

Despite my happy-go-lucky approach to life, I have experienced grief in my life. I lost a close friend when I was young. I have never been able to talk about it. This day would be no different. As the youngest person present, I was silent and respectful. I've felt the tears that have formed in some of our widow's eyes when they have listened to some of Sabrina's dealing with coming fresh from her husband's funeral. A part of me sees any deep feeling as beautiful; another part of me also fears such deep emotion.

Betty, a veteran of La Romita and grief added some thoughts of her own. "I think we all wonder if it is tougher for those left behind, of this we will never really know. For those of us who keep on living, we do have the ability to make good memories. Art fills our eyes with powerful visual images that can build strong memories. Creating art tests our imagination, which frees us from our physical limitations and allows us to transcend the ordinary routines of life. I know that everyone of our group is thankful that we have art in our lives and we are thankful to be around people who appreciate art. We are also very thankful of people like Mimi, who help art to become an even more positive experience in our lives. I hope that everyone can find a way to have more art in his or her life."

"Amen to that," added the art novice Jimmy.

It was Sabrina's turn to continue the discussion. "One thing that I have been surprised by, in this whole process of being the surviving spouse, is the shame."

"Shame?" I asked, not seeing how this emotion could be apart of grief.

"Oh yes, I know its ridiculous, but it is a powerful part of the healing. There is a certain shame in the feeling that your loss puts a burden on everyone around you."

"This I understand," added Joanne, our very wise, long distance traveler from Malaysia. "I have experienced this most human emotion, not only in the loss of my husband, I have had to confront this emotion many times in my charitable, non-profit work. It was the Peace Corps that originally took me to Malaysia. In developing countries, there are inevitable setbacks in this type of work. I learned early on that I had to deal with my grief in the losses of the people I loved. At first I would try to hide my grief and then it would infuse itself into my behavior, usually with bad consequences. Since I didn't deal with the emotions of loss, it would tend to burst out of me in ways that only made it worse. I would then not only feel the pain of the grief, but also the embarrassment and shame of not being able to deal with it. I learned to pray for those that we had lost and for myself. Then I could turn my pain into inspiration that would honor those who had crossed over to the other side."

This sobering observation left all of us silent and introspective. Omar T has never been big on introspection, so it seemed like a good time to lighten the atmosphere. "I too feel the emotion of grief with every woman who comes into my life and then I leave behind for the next beauty that presents herself to me." This allowed everyone to chuckle and let go of some of the heavy emotion. Though smiling, in a sign of gentle rebuke, Sabrina threw her sketchbook at me. Catching her act of humorous scolding, I just smiled and batted my eyelashes at her as Jimmy completely cracked up. In my final diversion tactic, I went on to proclaim, "Did you hear what's for dinner? Chicken scaloppini with lemons and olives." With this announcement, everyone did in fact begin to feel better.

Chapter 16 Fateful return to San Gemini

Edmund, knowing that I still had my rental car and possibly because he witnessed that I had be just moping around talking about grief with Sabrina, approached me with a favor request. "Omar, I wonder if I could impose on you to run a quick errand for me. The thought of running an errand in Umbria sounded more like a fun adventure than an imposition. Quickly, I had the filled out requested paperwork for the International Institute for Restoration and Preservation Studies lying next to me on my rental passenger seat. I made my way leisurely, making the normally 10 to 15 minute drive in more like 25 to 30 minutes. After all, for me this was adventure, not errand running. En route, the mood of talking grief with Sabrina had switched to something that I would describe as upbeat. At the time, I had no idea that fate was about to shine kindly on me, but perhaps I had a kind of premonition. I had thought that I was just happy to be doing something different, a chore that a local might be doing—not to mention that I saw nothing but incredible beauty and history all around me. I have always been rather taken with San Gemini as well. Edmund didn't even need to explain where to find the institute; I had noticed it on our previous visit. Edmund said that he had just gotten off of the phone with Gina, the lead restorer assigned to the La Romita project, who would be sitting at the front desk when I arrived. I parked and made my way up to the main square. I overcame the temptation to grab a gelato and a café, using some will power—I decided to return for treats after making the drop off. Again, you might wonder with all the pre-occupation with Italian coffee and Gelato. As I have already mentioned, the quality is tops. They are both also standards in even the smallest of hilltowns. Finally, there is the immensely important matter of feeling like a local, whenever you partake in these staples of their culture.

I headed slightly downhill on Via Roma. I did take in some of the interaction inside and outside of the shops of this heart of the city. The butcher leaned against his door, talking away with an elder that he has probably known his whole life. The florist leaned over, stroking a silver tipped, black terrier, patiently held by its human. Opera bounced around the barbershop, the rich tones of Placido Domingo spilled out of the door and warmed all of us who passed by. I continued to think that my good mood was just one of being on an adventure and that I was doing someone a favor at the same time. I had also been thinking on my drive and current stroll about all of the many wonderful Umbrian experiences that had already come my way. Given much time on my own, it is inevitable that any woman of current interest will come to mind. This of course included, Princess Catarina and especially our night out together in Terni. As playful as was that evening, she had been rather businesslike lately. Perhaps, she was reestablishing her posture in our relationship—or should I say superiority? It didn't really matter to me, I had a job to do for my father and whatever bit of Catarina that she was willing to share was just fine with me.

My Catarina trance was broken with my spotting of the entry to the Institute. Through the glass door, I could see a woman working away at the desk just inside the door. With her face pointing down at the papers in front of her, I had yet to realize my fortunate fate as I opened the door. When she looked up, I went into shock. I was looking upon the same soft, welcoming expression that I had locked onto outside of the Spoleto Opera House. The vision that had not only reentered my mind daily, it had become a part of my nightly dreams. Whenever I recalled this woman, I felt both an excitement at the comfort that I associated with her and a certain melancholy from the understanding that it was so unlikely that I would ever see her again. When I opened the door and saw the face of the woman that had been filling my constant visions, well, I was so in shock, that I was unable to speak.

She was so consumed in her work that at first, she did not notice anything unusual in my presence. As I entered, she did look up. Without really looking me over, she quickly figured that I must be Edmund's errand boy. In perfect English, she did what I was still unable to do, she spoke. "You must be Omar, and those papers in your hand must be for me, I'm Gina." Once she said her name, the same thing that had happened to me, seemed to give her a bit of a jolt. For a moment, she too remained silent, taking me in with a similar intensity that I assume was showing in my eyes. Finally, a recognition seemed to sink in. "Wait... I have seen you before... You were at the Opera... but then you disappeared."

It was time to get over the shock and respond to this wonderful moment of a very kind fate. Not only were we having the incredible good fortune of coming upon each other again, this time, instead of being lost within a crowd, it was just us in a small room. I took a deep breath as the reassurance of her also recognizing me, relaxed the situation. "I... thought I would never see you again..." Hearing the over intensity of my own words, I quickly tried to add something more normal. "I'm Omar." Then, remembering that she already stated my name, obviously getting it from Edmund, I blushed some more with embarrassment. To my surprise and I suppose also relief, I noticed that she also blushed.

Chapter 17 You got your moose

In the shock of actually meeting Gina, I took a deep breath and did my best to gather myself. I asked if I could join her in sitting down—she behind the desk, I in front. After our initial embarrassments, we relaxed and began to discover all of the incredible circumstances between our initial sighting of each other, how she was named the lead restorer for the La Romita fresco, how until now, we had missed each other on her previous visits to the school. She had even noticed my artwork tacked to the wall, next to the seat that I occupied when painting. She not only guessed which artwork was mine among all of the artists, she went on to describe some of my pieces—she was especially fond of my sketches of fellow students. Things were going so well that I boldly asked if she could join me for an afternoon gelato and either a coffee or a glass of wine to go with it. Without an additional word, she rose, placed the papers that I had brought, into a file and then said, "*andiamo*!" She suggested we try the Caffè Paretti, right around the corner. We started with gelato. She had tiramisu and vanilla. I had caramel and amaretto. We shared all four. We started with a café and then moved on to a glass of Orvieto *bianco*. Before I returned to La Romita, we knew many things about each other, including that neither of us was in a relationship. Ok, I know that you're wondering if my interactions with Catarina thus far would qualify as a relationship, but since such was clearly, unclear, I felt it appropriate not to mention it. To further excuse my lack of it being classified as such, Catarina had informed me that she was off to Paris and a wine show for two days. Thus, *principessa* was away and perhaps more telling toward the current discussion, she did not invite me along. Regardless of all of these complications, I left San Gemini smitten.

Dinner had already started when I returned to La Romita. Fortunately, my fellow students had not cleaned out the dinner platters. I plated up some pizza with Umbrian kale, Nduja salami, tomatoes, & Robiola cheese, accompanied with a delicious salad containing fresh pear and walnuts. As I made my way to an empty chair, bursting to fill in Jimmy and Sabrina on how fate had brought me to the mystery woman, I realized that there was some sort of crisis being discussed. There was no seat next to the dynamic duo, so I would have to inform them later. I sat with Barbara from Alaska, her sister Rosemary and her husband Bruce, as well as fellow Salt Lake City resident Flora. They were apparently discussing a phone message.

"You got your moose." This was the message to Barbara, from her son back in Alaska. No further explanation was offered. Our group had come from 10 different states of America, with a German and a Malaysian to give some additional perspective. In this era of cell phones, being so far away is perhaps not so far away anymore. Isn't it inevitable that when we go away for any extensive period that something goes wrong at home? There is the sudden leaky water pipe, the unexpected charge to our bank account, or the family member hurting themselves, perhaps something even worse. I suppose we might call that Murphy's Law. Perhaps in Italy they refer to a Guido law or some other common Italian name. My apologies, but I have a flighty mind that thinks about things like this—especially when filled with thoughts of a new beauty in my life.

Barbara read her note to us all, and then went silent. She let us begin to imagine the worse. We had visions of herding moose trampling down her garden or even her home. It was suggested that a moose might be some new app for her phone. Another student asked if there was such a thing as a moose club. Barbara didn't seem very upset for such a mysterious message, from a son some 5000 miles away. Once I caught an actual glint in her eye, I began to suspect that Barbara was having a little fun with all of us Alaska ignorant, mainlanders.

"Barbara," I asked, "Why do I think that you already know what the message means?"

She held her straight face for a little longer before finally beginning to chuckle a bit. A warm smile came to her face as she spoke.

"I suspect he bagged me a moose since I had asked him for one."

"Bagged you a moose?" Asked Flora.

"Yes, that means he shot me a moose."

"So that is a good thing, right?"

"Yes, but I may have to leave to carve-up the beast."

Soft spoken Flora, followed with a timid, "oh, I see."

Right then Barbara's phone blinked. I noticed that Barbara's sister Rosemary and husband Bruce both had an expression of amusement on their face.

"That is probably him," commented Barbara. "I asked him if I needed to get home fast."

We all waited for the response as Barbara's finger slowly pulled on the screen of her IPhone.

She chuckled as her eyes left her screen and looked upon all of us waiting for an answer to the fate of Barbara and her moose.

"He said not to be silly, he would take care of it."

There was a collective sigh of relief, or perhaps more of just a pleasant chuckle. Barbara's story had brought me back to being a part of the group, though I quickly returned to wondering if this very afternoon, Gina and I had just bagged our own figurative 'moose?' Was our moose each other?

Chapter 18 Labro

LABRO, Umbria

On our morning bus ride to the picturesque hilltown of Labro, I had time to contemplate the extraordinary circumstances around the meeting of Gina and how well we seemed to get along. Jimmy and Sabrina were in complete disbelief of how I had found Gina and that she had ironically already been to La Romita multiple times when we weren't there. Crazy. Now I knew she would be at La Romita when we returned for lunch—very reassuring. As we headed south to Labro, which is actually just across the border into the province of Lazio, we made a stop at the lakeside village of Lago di Piediluca. We got a little concerned when we realized that the whole town had practically shut down following its busy tourist season. That meant that there was no bathroom to be found for the ladies and no cappuccino for me. This left me a bit cranky.

Quickly we all took photos of Labro from the lakeside. The truly magical setting made me forget about the unavailability of a cappuccino and I was able to just enjoy the scene. Labro sits in the distance perched high above the lake. On this day the morning light danced off the lake exposing a variety of color and texture. You could actually make out different currents, swirling with shapes of silver, gray and a charcoal blue. Off of the right bank, there is a grove of tall deciduous trees that were a mix of greens and some fall yellows. As the earth rises from the valley there is a hillside of lush green oak trees before giving way to yet a higher slope that still has clusters of oaks but also exposed stone and hay colored grasses. The stone fortress of Labro sits on top like a pale pistachio gelato on top of its cone. To our relief, trusty bus driver, Raniero, swooped us off to a nearby roadside *gelateria caffè* with *bagno*. While the ladies lined up for the bathroom, Jimmy and I sat down for a cappuccino. Ah the simple pleasures. Sabrina joined us and asked, "Is it too early for a gelato?" We decided it was never too early. Especially since I had been imagining how Labro looked like a giant scoop of this creamy treat.

Walking the streets of Labro, you get a mix of its storied past, along with an excitement of its current renewal. Much of Labro has been remodeled recently. Some Dutch architects purchased most of the town and have helped to refurbish it. Most of the side streets or what is better referred to as pathways, seem so quiet most of the time that we all wondered, "do people in fact live here?" As I wandered off exploring, some Vivaldi snuck out of one of the windows and danced around the stone nooks and crannies. More magic. For those of us who reached the top we were rewarded with beautiful views and a chance to meet Jerry and Karen from the Tahoe/Reno area. They were staying in the monastery down the road on a work & stay program. Their adventure turned out not to be the best match for this 40-50 year old couple. Their work was to assist through cleaning, making supply runs, and helping to feed a group of performers. They ended up with a group of really young people, sleeping in a tent and wondering what they were doing there? When we found them, they were enjoying a moment away from their 'simple' life, feeling the sun on their faces, in a spot with a spectacular view. We enjoyed talking with them and later felt guilty for not kidnapping them to our beautiful retreat. Tripod is the name we fondly gave the black and white wiry dog, who made Labro his home. He has but 3 legs. Tripod seems to spend his day showing off that being short one leg has not affected him at all. He kept showing up wherever I was. He was always smiling, panting and moving at his steady and persistent speed. It appeared that all morning long, he was doing laps around the ups and downs of Labro. He slipped and slid around a bit like the rest of us taking on the obstacles of a hilltown, but with the same kind of determination as those of us searching out beauty, Tripod kept moving forward.

Sabrina and I also met a most friendly cat. This beauty of orange and white, loved being rubbed all over and rubbing up against anyone who paid him or her attention. Diana from Ketchum Idaho joined us and took a lot of photos of the cat and me, rustling around in a momentary love fest. Everyone in our group loved how picturesque Labro was, though several thought it too quiet and remote to spend much time there. I, on the other hand, imagined parking myself for 6 months and writing a novel and routinely visiting the town's 5 restaurants. Bliss! This I expressed out loud. What I did not share was that I was imagining Gina being my co-habitant in a love dwelling.

Upon our return, I had a nice visit with Gina before lunch. She showed me the work that she had performed on the fresco that morning and discussed her plan going forward. I kept my feelings about the similarity that I felt with the work of Giotto to myself. I did not want to sound like an idiot to my new expert of a friend. The naked man, in the lower right corner, with a face that Catarina had titled as angry, was now almost completely exposed. Now that his face was cleaned up, we thought it more an expression of anguish. Then, there was the face of the man that the naked man seemed to be engaged with. Now that Gina had cleaned up his face, I made the comment that it looked like an expression of contempt. Gina agreed with me. There seemed to be separate hillsides rising separately on both sides of the figures. Gina pointed out what was clearly some kind of structures on top of these background hillsides—some more unveiling should clarify this. Gina also felt that the second figure with the contempt face was probably either royal, an authority from the church or a rich man. This conclusion was drawn from his exposed fine shoes and what was something around his head. She was very anxious to expose the rest of this by tomorrow. All of our discussion had been taking place within the intimacy of her little tarp cave. As interesting as all this was, I just kept thinking about how I wanted to take her up into my arms and hold her, kiss her. I did focus myself and kept a gentlemanly distance—though we did inadvertently rub against each other a few times and this felt rather electric. Next was lunch of an amazing Minestrone soup. We did of course sit next to each other at lunch and our conversation stayed fluid and easy. I did my best to avoid looking over at Sabrina and Jimmy, who it seemed, had strategically placed themselves at the next table with the view of us. When I did catch their glances, they were smiling and perhaps even giggling a bit.

Chapter 19 Stroncone and Bruno

I got in a visit with Gina before we headed off to the hilltown of Stroncone. She was already at work when I wandered into the studio. She looked so cute in her working glasses and hat. Not accessories we would normally associate with making someone look adorable, but what can I say, I was smitten with this woman. She had uncovered what appeared, even to this layman, as a cardinal's hat. "No doubt about it," stated Gina, "our mystery man is a cardinal." I couldn't help but think about how my time in Italy has been filled with precious mysteries—people, places and a fresco.

The night before I had confessed my feelings about Gina to my mother and filled her in on the whole story of how we had met. Mother, being the one spiritual member of our family, via meditation, and a rather unique connection to the cosmos, was not surprised by what to me seemed like such an amazing series of events. "It was obviously meant to be Omar. I must say, I like the way you two feel together."

"Thanks Ma." I paused a moment before asking the rather obvious follow up. And Catarina?

She actually started to chuckle. This at first made me feel a little apprehensive, but it was such a warm chuckle that I ended up joining in. Her mature giggles ended with just a loving smile. "You and Catarina were clearly not meant to be a long term relationship Omar. That being said, I hope you have had some fun and learned some things in the time you spent with her?"

You just can't take anything personal when discussing anything with my mother. She is so full of loving thoughts toward everyone and so content within herself. She relaxes everyone around her.

"Yes mother, it was very fun having a princess of wine put her arm around mine, to witness how people reacted to her, and how they reacted to me, being the man at her side." I then paused, thinking about the second part of her statement. "Mother, what did you mean did I learn from her? Did you mean as far as the winery and Dad's possible investment?"

"Oh no Omar, you know that I take no interest in your father's investing. I meant in learning something about life. If we are not learning my boy, we are just deteriorating."

Equal to mother's ability to relax those of us lucky enough to be around her, is her ability to challenge how we see life. This put me into deeper thought, something which is not necessarily natural for me.

After quite some time in thought, I finally responded to the spiritual guide of my family.

"Yes mother, I have learned quite a bit. First of all, Catarina has been a reminder to never judge a book solely by the cover." As usual, Ma was her typical good listener. She patiently waited for me to form and express my thoughts. "Catarina's presence is so commanding that it is easy to forget that she is still just a person like you and me. She still sees things uniquely, she still feels awkward on occasion, and she still has to sleep at night." What I thought, but didn't express out loud, was that during sex she also talks dirty and moans with the strength of Catherine of Siena.

STROGONE, UMBRIA
Deamer
ARTBZ.BZ

Stroncone has many things to love, especially how so many of the community gather and loiter in the main piazza. Just watching them, let alone sketching them, makes you feel a part of something beyond being a tourist. We were all happy to see the piazza bustling with an open market on the day of our visit. Like a lot of the hilltowns that have a market, the collection of venders is quite diverse. Today's venders included a housewares dealer, a seller of all kinds of chairs, a linen/fabric seller, a cheese seller with gorgeous wheels of all kinds of cheese, a woman's clothes seller with a very odd selection and a shoe seller with an amazing number of shoes. A flower seller made an early stop and a fishmonger made an appearance for about an hour around noon. The *caffè* on the piazza was busy all day putting out coffees for the shoppers and our group of working artists. A lot of sketches were produced in our half-day visit to Stroncone. Not only was there all of the activity of the piazza, the town is filled with quaint scenes and spectacular views. Shaped in an oval like a smaller Orvieto, Stroncone commands a strong presence. Most of its historic exterior wall has survived, though with many repairs. This makes its footprint feel grander than those cities that have lost much of the walls that gave them a first line of defense. Stroncone reminds us that the creation of hilltowns was a matter of defense, not to enjoy the beautiful views that we find so endearing today. One thing I love about Stroncone is how unique are its paths and sections. Despite its size, there is a sense of a variety of community neighborhoods around its various piazzas and viewpoints. It is a really fun town to walk around and not too demanding as much of the town is on a kind of plateau, making the ups and downs not so severe. I also liked the sense of town pride with its community black and red flags found throughout the town. There were a number of peaceful places to pull up to and sketch or to just imagine what it would be like to live here. I was particularly intrigued by a couple of decrepit but incredibly scenic houses facing the mostly uninhabited lush green mountains rising on Stroncone's west side. Once again my imagination wandered, seeing myself living and remodeling one of this scenic abodes. I imagined spending half a day on the remodel, while working the other half of the day on doing art and making love to Gina. Of course there would have to be time made for lengthy meals and cappuccino/gelato breaks as well. Speaking of gelato, our group had just about completely wiped out the remaining stock of the café's gelato. It was a two-cappuccino morning for me. It is a glorious thing to start and finish a hilltown with a cappuccino, and yes, I had some gelato too. Both my mother and I were fond of the lemon and melon combo that we chose from their remaining 4 flavors. And, the community around the *caffè* was a delight. Several of us had some interaction with the locals, whether just a greeting or two, or something more substantial. Sabrina, as usual, outdid us all. She met Bruno, who was so friendly that we would later crown him the town's ambassador. Bruno, like so many of us, took an instant liking to Sabrina, which resulted in her getting in a private tour. He unlocked doors and paraded her around, telling her stories of the history of Stroncone as well as what was happening now—a personal tour guide. Bruno was a personification of how Stroncone is a very beautiful and friendly town.

Over an amazing lunch of fried squash blossoms and puff pastry tarts, Gina glowed with how she had unveiled some more of the fresco background and that there were definitely structures on the hillside. "And there is something familiar about them." I asked if she had exposed any more of the cardinal, pun intended. She giggled and said, "No, it is going to be perhaps the trickiest operation. It will probably be the last act of the restoration."

Chapter 20 Spello and Trevi

Spello starts on the valley floor and then winds its way up its hilltown slope at a fairly dramatic pace. Fortunately, our bus was able to drop us off at the top and all of our exploring was for the most part, downhill. That was the good news. The bad news was that the traffic on the main, but still narrow roads, could be quite active and intimidating. Just ask Mary Jeane, from Washington D.C., who got quite lost—but don't worry, we found her. Like almost all the hilltowns, it is really easy to get turned around and lost. All of the stone buildings and their nooks and crannies can start to look like the ones that you just saw a minute ago. This combined with how the pathways meander up, down and sideways, can really throw off the internal compass. Sometimes, getting lost can be an opportunity that leads you to some unexpected prize.

On top of the usual navigational challenges, Spello had a big section of its main road torn up for a new sewer system. That being said, Spello is very scenic and has some exceptional nooks for creative loitering. The grandness of Spello's gates of entry, take you back in time—they have a real medieval feel. To my delight, Gina took the morning off so that she could show us the frescos of Spello's three churches. Access to the public was apparently, normally limited—as the restorer she had keys. My mother, Jimmy and Sabrina tagged along. In particular, we took a close look at the Perugino and Pinturicchio frescos as they were both completed in the early 1500's; near the time that La Romita became a monastery. Yes, these are the same two fellows that I keep confusing for each other. Perugino, "Big P's" work, like our fresco, I found to not be overly religious or symbol dominated. However, we all agreed that his work still felt different from our revealing fresco. The Pinturicchio, "Little P," cycle includes the *Annunciation*, the *Nativity* and the *Dispute with the Doctors*, plus four *Sibyls* in the vault. I took a long look at Pinturicchio's Nativity scene. There were parts of it that had a similarity, but the overall impression was that it had little in common with our fresco. I laugh, in my head, every time I make a claim on "our fresco." I guess you could say that being there for its initial unveiling, all of the research that I've done and the mystery behind it, had made me feel rather personally attached to it. Not to mention that it was now linked to Gina, whom I also wanted to be linked. While inside the Chiesa di S. Maria Maggiore, Gina made sure that we all took our eyes off of the frescos long enough to look at the floor. "The floor tiles were all made in nearby Deruta, where the ancient tradition continues today." After our church tour, Gina bid us adieu, heading back to La Romita and our blossoming child of a wall. Sad to see her leave, but somewhat relieved to no longer feel my mother, Jimmy and Sabrina staring at Gina and my every move. It was comforting to know that I would see her later.

Every town should have a Forno Artigiano to greet its visitors. The amazing aromas that squeeze out the entry of this bakery, sneak around the nearby stone pathways and wrap around a travelers senses like a warm hug and friendly smile. We had lunch reservations but discovering Bar Giardino almost destroyed the plan. Since its amazing terrace dining is rather hidden from the Bar's rather low profile front, not to mention that it was in the current construction zone, it would have been easy to walk right by. But fortunately my mother and I discovered it because yours truly was ready for a cappuccino. Mother, being mother, is pretty much always eager to join me in whatever sounds good as far as food and beverages. Thus my nose led us to the Bar Giardino espresso machine, which led us to their courtyard, which took our breath away. Incredible views of the Olive tree covered nearby hills and lush accompanying Umbrian mountains—all this in an open, flowering courtyard, hidden from the bustle of the center of Spello. And to my mother's delight a *bagno* too. As a bonus, while ordering I got to witness a scene that takes place all over the world. A couple of the Bar's family, whether an actual family member, a regular, or former employee, had brought in their baby boy to show him off. Common to any culture, in any location, everyone stops and takes in the miracle of birth with a smile and an ah. I got a photo so that I could sketch the scene later.

It was tough getting up and leaving this sanctuary, but we had been promised an exceptional meal at restaurant La Cantina. It did not disappoint. Hand crafted food with tall stemware, filled with lush Umbrian wine. For a while, I even forgot about Gina. Nonetheless, knowing that she would be at La Romita when we returned helped to keep me from heading back to Bar Giardino for gelato and some more peaceful meditation. (The novel cover is of the town of Spello).

"La Cantina"
SPELLO UMBRIA   Pearson ARTOZ, 82

Trevi is one of those hilltowns that would qualify as worthy of a Disney set. Even without Gina at my side, Trevi made for a wonderful afternoon adventure. Not only does Trevi command a prominent place within this rich historic valley, it is one of those medieval towns that makes its way rather up the slope in a circular, symmetrically, scenic manner. Fortunately, access is from near the top so that we didn't have to navigate the severity from the lower defense walls. Equaling the views of Trevi from below are the views from Trevi of the valley and the neighboring hilltowns. Not to be overlooked is how wonderful are all of the crannies and nooks of the meandering cobblestone pathways. Trevi will fill up any camera quickly. The Chiesa of San Francisco is the pillar of the town's churches and includes an adjoining museum. I found the somewhat hidden *chiesa*, Sant' Emiliano very endearing, serene—the architecture, the art, everything has a rather soothing spirituality. I found the exterior courtyard in front of Caffè Roma inspiring for my sketchbook. The patrons had perfectly spaced themselves— an excellent composition. One of Trevi's festivals is for their black celery. No, it does not have the look of black licorice. Black celery still resembles its green cousin, with its green being a little darker and more opaque than the bright version. I found Sabrina trying on some beautiful hand made scarfs. I encouraged her to go for it and she did. Her new sash of color looked brilliant next to her radiant smile. Watch out locals, here comes Sabrina to be your new friend. I convinced Alfredo, our substitute driver for the day, to take us to the road around the neighboring monastery so that we could photograph the so scenic Trevi from its perfect viewpoint. I earned some bonus points from the group for that idea. Although I was very pleased with the lack of responsibility in my assistant role, I did feel that I needed to make an occasional contribution.

TREVI- UMBRIA

ARTbZ.EZ

Gina agreed to join us for dinner upon our return. Once again Egizia and Franca, the La Romita cooks, had created a fabulous feast of breaded chicken breasts with succulent organic tomatoes and arugula. I always laugh to myself when I use words like local and organic in Italy. These terms, which have come to mean quality in America, are irrelevant here. For centuries, local and organic have been their only way of life. Try to explain the American movement toward local and organic and you'll end up with a very perplexed Umbrian face, asking something like, "You mean that there are people who eat food that isn't local, that comes from a thousand or more miles away?"

I was starting to believe that Gina was enjoying my company as much as I was enjoying her. She showed me what were clearly some lone trees in the fresco and informed me that we would have a clearer look at them after her work the next day. I smiled and stated, "It is so fun sharing this adventure with you." I'm not certain, given the muted light under her tarp, but I believe she blushed.

Chapter 21 Todi and a Special Wine

Todi is one of the Umbrian cities that attract a fair amount of non-Italians to reside there (it was once named one of the world's most livable cities). It has enough size and services to be more than just a place to hide from the rest of the world. Todi is perched on a tall two-crested hill overlooking the east bank of the river Tiber. Yes, this is the same river that famously flows through Rome and onto the Mediterranean. There are commanding distant views in every direction, which are accessed from a variety of special locations. Todi is also well known for its free funicolare, which lifts you from a convenient parking area to the height of the main walking paths—all of this through a beautiful forest of rich and diverse green trees, bushes and flowering plants. Once walking the streets of Todi, you will notice how well tourists and locals mix, as well as how diverse are its shops and restaurants. The adjoining piazzas of Popolo and Garibaldi, are one of those breathtaking Italian city centers. All the well-portioned Gothic and renaissance buildings surrounding all of the open people space is stunning. The ancient stonework is brought to life with the color and good cheer of the accompanying businesses and restaurants. The bright and friendly *caffè* and restaurants on the west side, look squeezed out of the ancient buildings, like the shiny-striped colors of a kid's toothpaste. The exclamation mark is the crown of the north end of the piazza, the *Cattedrale*, which is accessed by a monumental flight of stone steps. For mother, and myself, the lure of Caffè Serrani's cappuccino, gelato and its colorful outdoor seating in the middle of Piazza Popolo, was a grander draw than any fresco study on this day. I did make the climb up the steps and enjoyed a quick self-guided tour of the Cathedral. The view back on the piazza is truly magnificent. I also made my way through the somewhat crazed parked cars of the Piazza di Garibaldi to check out the spectacular views to the east. In 1849, Guiseppe Garibaldi turned to Todi as a home and sanctuary after his failed attempt of bringing democracy to the Republic of Rome. He is considered, with Camillo Benso, Count of Cavour, Victor Emmanuel II and Giuseppe Mazzini, as one of Italy's "fathers of the fatherland." While in Italy, you rarely have to go far to receive a reminder of these men's contribution to the unification of Italy. Virtually every city is littered with streets, piazzas and buildings bearing their names. Garibaldi's larger than life statue, stands in the middle of the piazza of his name, though a close up look can be hazardous. There is a constant battle of mini cars, trying for the few, precious surrounding parking spots. The double piazza, center of town, is so glorious that many never get around to walking around the other streets of Todi—I suspect that the locals appreciate this. That being said, there are many wonderful roads and pathways throughout this diverse hilltown. I left my ma behind. She was having a blast sketching people, both those sitting near her and those walking by. I wandered downhill, twisting and turning through winding pathways that quietly whispered of the past. I discovered a path around the lower perimeter—the views looking up, rivaled the view from atop.

Jimmy and Sabrina made the adventurous climb up into the tower of the Tempio di San Fortunato. According to Jimmy, "It was more like we were intruding on the center of Todi's pigeon population, than climbing a historic human creation. That being said, there were some cool views from the top." Just getting to San Fortunato is a climb in itself. Thus I passed on going up to the tower. I was content with a quick walk around the interior. Before returning down to the funicolare to the parking area, I decided that I deserved a gelato treat from Il Fondaco, *doppio cioccolato*. The adjacent park is a magnificent spot for loitering with a cup of gelato. There are views looking back on Todi, of the villas and farmland below and my fellow loiterers. There was an interesting mix of locals, our artist group, and some other tourists. Peering over the wall, I found two villas that looked particularly attractive. I took a photo of each so that I could later discuss with Sabrina and Jimmy, on which one would be a better purchase for us—need to feed the dream, don't you think? It would be a tough choice between the one with the pool and the one with the olive orchard. A little further in the distance was an intoxicating scene of two red tractors, moving slowly through a field of bright yellow sunflowers. I couldn't wait to return to La Romita to describe this vision to Gina. My thought was that after staring at a wall and its intimate painted details all day, a description of such beauty, in the Italian countryside, should be a welcome diversion.

Alas, there were other plans for my afternoon. It was time for a return to Senza Speranza. Just as I finished my last bite of gelato, up pulled Enrico—no, not in a Ferrari. He was in a small truck—the always-working member of the family. On the drive to the winery, it was confirmed that Catarina would be waiting for us. Catarina and I had exchanged a couple of emails since our night in Terni—the night where I was introduced to the power of Catarina's pleasure vocabulary. She had been a little flirty but each email also contained information from Enrico to pass on to my father. Thus, not only were my feelings growing toward Gina, Catarina was keeping her feelings closely guarded. I smiled to myself as Enrico and I exchanged pleasantries. First of all, I was happy to again be in his presence. I just liked him. No pretentiousness and interesting—Enrico is just a good guy. Secondly, I was very curious to see how I would feel to be back in the presence of the great Catarina. Not just to see how she treated me after our night of seduction, but also to see how my feelings toward Gina would influence my lustful thoughts of Catarina.

My father had emailed me a checklist to go through with the heirs of the winery. Enrico and I hashed it out rather quickly. Rather than being in the stuffy office, I had suggested that we sit down inside the cool of the winery and enjoy a glass of wine while we had our discussion. As suspected, he liked the idea of us being in his lair, his *querencia*, his place of comfort. I also thought that a glass of good vino might help me, as well, with facing the daunting Catarina. On our drive to Torgiano, I spoke to Enrico about my concept of Senza Speranza having a pricy signature wine such as Lungarotti had with its Rubesco. I was not all that surprised when he said that he had already created one. "Again the board was against it, so I went ahead and created one with my own money. I have five vintages now, none of it bottled. I think we have something special already."

"What's the grape blend Enrico?"

"Same as Lungarotti's Rubesco Riserva Vigna Monticchio, Sangiovese and Canaiolo and a touch of Sagrantino. Just as there are the Super Tuscans, which blend Cabernet Sauvingnon with Sangiovese, our Sangiovese and Canaiolo are made for each other. By adding the tannins and structure of Sagrantino, I think that we have our Super Umbrian." My mouth started to water with just the suggestion of getting some of his special wine on my palate. "It's not just me

Omar, there are several other Umbrian wine makers talking about this wine becoming a signature for our region. This idea was held back while there became more history and production of the Sagrantino grape."

"I'm not familiar with Sagrantino."

"It is indigenous to Umbria and it has some of the highest tannic acid levels of any grape variety used to make wine. As you know Omar, even though we try to emphasize the fruit and other flavors that we associate with it being delicious, without an acidic backbone, wines are just flabby. The origins of the grape are widely disputed, but what is known is that it was used primarily for dessert wines for many years, the grape being dried in the *passito* style, much like a Recioto di Valpolicella. It is its history as a sweet wine, associated with friars and the sacrament that christened it Sagrantino. Beginning in 1976, however, the wines were also made in a dry style, and that is how they are primarily produced today."

"In fact this discussion fits perfectly into an activity I would like to take you on. I want to take you to Montefalco, show it to you and specifically visit Arnoldo Caprai, they are responsible for taking this difficult grape with a history as only a sweet wine and developing its characteristics into a table wine with incredible aging potential." That sounded like an adventure right up my alley.

I was not surprised that Catarina had not been awaiting our arrival. It would appear that the princess protocol demanded her entrance to be late. We had finished all of my father's questions and were into tasting the third vintage of Enrico's special wine, when in pranced Catarina. Stunning as always, today's boots were maroon leather, tight at the ankle with its higher body resembling a hound dog's folded skin layers. Mini skirt, leaving a lot of exposed leg and thigh for me to reminisce about. Her blouse matched the skirt in color and the boots in look. It had clumped folds like the boots on both sides of her neck to her shoulders, then sleeveless. It came tight to her chest, exposing the upper half of her amazing breasts. It then got real loose below her chest flowing back and forth with her hips as she did her strut in our direction.

As I stood to greet her, I felt a little lightheaded. I wasn't sure if it was the wine or the return to being in her formable presence. We did the obligatory three cheek kisses; she then commanded Enrico and me to return to our seats. "Text me when you are finished with him Enrico. I have something planned for us." With that, she abruptly turned and strutted back out, undoubtedly knowing my eyes would be taking in every one of her hip swings. When I turned my attention back to Enrico, he was giving me a very bemused look. A look that I am sure he has had a lot of practice, sharing with any male who has the fortune of watching Catarina leave a room. Seeing his expression, I too smiled and soon we were both chuckling.

His look got more serious and then he decided to take on the new elephant in the room. "My sister's affairs are of course none of my business but since we are also conducting business together, I should let you know that despite what you may think, her interest in you has little to do with our business. Her interest in a man is never out of some loyalty to the winery. That is just not her style. That being said, you should also know that Catarina has never shown interest in only one man, at any one time, at least not yet."

I kept eye contact with Catarina's wise and good-hearted brother, nodding my head up and down, confirming that I understood his message and that I had already pretty much concluded the same sentiments.

"Now," he broke the silence of neither of us knowing what else would be appropriate to discuss as far as his sister. "Let's try the fourth vintage of the wine." For each of our glasses, he obtained our wine with what is known as a thief, a vessel that you can slip into a barrel of wine and pull out the liquid. As a veteran of this practice, Enrico never spilled a drop. Since the fourth vintage showed its youthful age, it was very tight. I decided to use a trick that I had witnessed from a restaurant/wine maker, Walter Georis, back in my home county of Monterey, California. I picked up an unused fork from our accompanying cheese tray, stuck it in the glass and proceeded to dash it back and forth, forcing some much needed oxygen into the wine.

Enrico's bemused expression again appeared. He then asked for the fork so that he could try this vulgar but effective technique. "Wow, better." We both took our time smelling and tasting. Hints of Eucalyptus had joined the emergence of the berry flavors of black current and perhaps even some blueberry. "Wow," this time it was my turn to add the ageless metaphor that gives you time to form your thoughts behind its expression. Finally I added, "This vintage has real potential Enrico."

"I agree." With that, he picked up his wine thief and headed to the latest vintage, the final of our tasting of the first five vintages. When he returned with another pair of perfectly poured glasses, I moved from my father's list to the question of the greatest curiosity to me.

"You haven't really explained what happened with your father Enrico. Is he still alive?"

"Yes Omar, he is still alive. But…, well…, he is not right in his mind."

"Is he in an institution?"

Enrico took a big sip, maybe even a gulp of his wine before he continued. "No, he is not in a formal institution. He is in a prison of his own mind. He still lives at our home. He gets up each day, eats his breakfast and then leaves the house for the rest of the day. What you have to understand is that he was so traumatized by our mother's death that his mind completely removed him from his previous life. He has no recognition of Catarina, the winery or myself. I don't think he actually knows who is our cook/housekeeper, the woman who makes him his meals. He never speaks her name. He just sits down, eats, says thank you and then leaves the house until exactly 1pm when he shows up for lunch. He then takes a nap and then leaves the house again until exactly 8pm when he returns."

"Even on bad weather days?"

"Yes."

"And you say he doesn't know you or Catarina?"

"That's right. He is courteous, always a gentleman, whenever we cross paths, but each time he treats us like it is the first time that we have met. Sometimes, he even introduces himself."

"I'm sorry Enrico, that has to be difficult."

"It is what it is Omar. We have lived with the situation for twenty years. Doctors say that it is some kind of selective amnesia. We tried for about five years to wake him out of it in many different ways, without any success. And now, well I'm quite certain that his life before is buried too deep to ever be found. We have even taken to calling him Sir, instead of Dad, hoping to avoid any confusion."

We both were quiet for a while, sipping our wine and contemplating the injustice of it all, until Enrico continued. "Thing is, if you met him in a casual situation, you would probably think that he is a perfectly normal, old, retired man. He goes about our town and speaks to anyone who speaks to him. It is very strange, in that he goes to the same places for coffee, a gelato or just to sit on one of the town benches. He visits the *Cattedrale* every day. But just like with us, he recognizes no one. Everyone that he meets, in his mind, he is meeting them for the first time. Francesca, our housekeeper, manages his clothes after he has gone to sleep. We have several copies of each thing that he wears. She lays out the same outfit every night with exactly five euro coins in his pants pocket."

I leaned back and let out the breath I had been holding in as I listened to this incredible story. Then, I had a flash back. "Wait, maybe I have met him. Does he hang out by the *Torre di Guardia?* He even has a key to the tower."

"Yes and yes. Did he let you in, insist you go to the top for the view?"

"Yes, incredible."

"It is rather an amazing story, isn't it?"

"It most certainly is…"

Chapter 22 Catarina's Toy

I really enjoyed my time with Enrico. He is just a good egg. Now, as far as the rest of the afternoon and early evening with Catarina, well, I am a bit hesitant to inform you that there was some more adult play involved. I know what you are thinking, "How can he when he has fallen for Gina?" Such condemnation is deserved. What can I say? I am of the weaker gender and whatever Catarina wants, she seems to get. I was all prepared to be nothing but professional with her. I had even prepared a list of business questions that I could specifically ask her, to help keep things from drifting into the amorous zone. You must understand that advance thinking is not very natural for me so hopefully you will give me some kudos, at least for having appropriate intentions. As usual, Catarina had her own agenda, and my intentions dissolved along with my resolve. I had a feeling that I was in trouble the moment that I reported to her. She grabbed me by the hand and literally pulled me out of the winery and into her Ferrari. Zoom, we were off to what is known in the trade as a vineyard house. These have become more and more popular in the winery world—a house hidden within the romance of the vineyards that wineries use as a promotional tool, to help boost their sales. As we

slid in a cloud of dust to the Senza Speranza hideaway, I
pretty much knew that my romantic heart didn't stand a
chance. The aged stone structure was covered with vines of
its own. Unlike the surrounding vineyards, these vines
blossomed with color. There were orange and red trumpet
shaped flowers, mixed with the scents of white jasmine.
There were modern touches of huge glass windows outlined
and enhanced by sleek metal work. Inside was cozy, filled
with way too many accessories conducive to seduction. It
all started with wine, wine and more wine. I was already
weakened from the vintage tasting of Enrico's signature
wine. Catarina poured some big glasses of red and then
went into a little speech on how my father should purchase
the vineyard and keep her and Enrico on as partners. This
all made sense, I had been thinking along the same lines.
What made it difficult for me to do anything other than nod
my head in agreement was that as she spoke, she was also
removing pieces of clothing. It was like punctuation to her
sentences. She would state a line and then a boot, a piece of
jewelry or something more revealing, would be tossed
aside, making all her comments end in an exclamation
mark. She finished everything that she had to say at the
same time she was completely naked. It was kind of like
reading a business letter where the sender finishes a

sentence with three exclamation points. Such overindulgence makes one forget what was the point. Also, as I believe I have mentioned before, every point of Catarina is wonderful. Like all her men, and I was certain there were others, I was putty in her hands. In fact, I was such a pile of putty that once she had finished undressing herself; she had to do the removing of my clothes as well. Once she had pulled me against her naked body, I was able to respond and forget about everything but the amazingness of the female form, especially this particular form. Catarina did not seem to notice, or care, about my lack of initial enthusiasm. She did just fine ordering me around and going into her forceful verbalization of Italian exclamations. Most of our play was a blur, as she drove me back to La Romita. What was clear, was how she confirmed my intuition and Enrico's subtle warnings. She let me know that the next day, she was off to Paris with another man, a count. She not only announced this to me with no regrets, she also added, "I hope you are not the jealous type, for I think that I will always have more than one man in my life."

Part of me was still feeling the bliss of intimate interaction with the temple that is woman, another part wanted to scream out that I too was interested in another woman. This stayed silently in my head. I did have a moment where I ironically identified with what was all too common of a female complaint. I did in fact feel a little like Catarina's toy. I also knew that she considered me expendable.

To help cleanse my mind, after tucking in my always so content mother, I put on my headphones and played some comfort music. Do you have some music that you go to when you want some reassurance? I have more than one, being in Italy; the choice was one of my favorite voices, singing in Operatic Italian. It doesn't hurt that this singer is also beautiful. I discovered the music of Emma Shapplin, in the movie The Fifth Element, the Luc Besson's colorful Sci-Fi movie, starring Bruce Willis and Milla Jovovich. The blue skinned futuristic superstar, "The Diva," sings a rock Opera, with the vocals supplied by Emma. This inspired me to look her up on Wikipedia and YouTube. Some combination of her history, artistic risk taking and a blessed voice, has really endeared her to me. Though rarely, do I understand the words within her work, I find myself often moved to the point of tears. As I drifted off in an Omar T type slumber, I dreamed that I was in one of the singer's eclectic videos. Reminiscent of Catarina, the other women in the video were chasing me around, trying to take off my clothes.

Chapter 23 Marmore Falls

I awoke feeling missing Gina pains. Yesterday had been the first day that I had not seen her since our fateful introduction. My pains of guilt for my romp with Catarina of course complicated these pains. I am pretty good at letting guilt slide right off of me, thus I just let it fall to the floor and worked on my happy anticipation of seeing Gina. I was also eager for an update on her progress with the fresco. That being said, my body and mind were still a little worn out from my time with Catarina. I was slow getting out of bed and joining the group for breakfast. Gina had yet to arrive. Our group actually had a light day planned, which was a perfect transition for me. It would give a little more distance between my time with Catarina and some more time with Gina. I also knew that Catarina would be in Paris for at least several days, which helped me let go of her and allowed me to now give my full attention to Gina. She still had not arrived before we left for our visit to Marmore falls, so I slipped into her tarp cave around the fresco and left her a note which simply said, "Missed you yesterday, looking forward to seeing you and getting updated on the fresco's progress. P.s., I didn't look this morning, I want to see it through your eyes first." I debated on how to sign it, your friend, sincerely, love… I settled on, "hugs Omar."

Have you ever heard of a spectacular waterfall that can be turned on and off by a switch? I had not and you can imagine my surprise when I learned the largest waterfall in Umbria and one of the largest in all of Europe, has an on/off switch. The only thing on the agenda, on this restful day, was a visit to the nearby Marmore Falls. We had caught a glimpse of the falls when driving by them on our way to other towns so that most of us were eager to visit them. They are spectacular. A relatively new feature is the walkways, which allow you to walk up the hillside, crossing some of the falls waterways and a closer view and feel of the falls. Closer meaning you have to be willing to get at least a little wet as the breeze and mist from the falls swirls all around you. The power that this falling water creates is amazing. To see and feel the powerful wind created by the falls is another beautiful reminder of the power and awe of nature—even if controlled by a switch. The Romans created the falls as part of their quest of bringing water from the mountains to their growing populations. Its flow is turned on and off, according to a published schedule, to satisfy the needs of tourists and the power company alike. It was kind of fun to go to a local tourist attraction. Besides our group, I saw only Italians, which gave us kind of an insiders feeling. With the exception of Assisi and to some degree Orvieto, I found Umbria so free of tourists that it felt like everything was very unaffected by tourism. In the hilltowns of Umbria, visits feel like a special insiders' ticket to a life so different from what we know in America. A life, which still reflects a past, so very rich in history and so filled with community. Unlike large tourist attractions, walking through these communities makes me reflect not only on the lives of the residents but also on the life I live.

The sound of the falling water at Marmore is powerful enough to eliminate the sounds of conversations or any other distractions. So even though there can be a lot of people around, you still feel a kind of one and one bond with this dramatic environment. I loved the sound so much that I recorded some video thinking that maybe these soothing sounds could help me fall asleep or meditate, once back to the reality of my life in America. My favorite moment was ordering a cappuccino and sipping it at a table near the edge, while layers of mist kept splashing across my face. Something about hearing the sound of the water falling, while sipping the hot frothy beverage and feeling the delicate but cool mists, was very tantalizing.

The mists and beauty of this dramatic water show, cleansed me of Catarina and prepared me for Gina. Before leaving, I picked some flowers to bring to Gina. After a short debate in my head, I decided to pick some from the cultivated garden rather than the wild flowers—it seemed like the least of two evils. Such debates, for better or worse, are common in the head of yours truly. Jimmy and Sabrina teased me about my collection. No, I had not filled them in on my afternoon with the wine princess. Over breakfast, I spoke only of Enrico's special wine and that I really hoped that my father could make a deal with the winery that would keep Enrico and Catarina as partners. I also picked up a bottle of a local vino at the little market/snack shop, adjacent to the falls ticket/gift shop. The purchase made me feel better about stealing some of their flowers…

ERNI UMBRIA

I slipped into Gina's cave with the flowers, the wine and a kiss on both of her dusty cheeks. This brought on a bit of dust spitting, which made us both laugh, which set a good mood for our reunion. Yes, with certain people, at certain moments, a one-day hiatus can make for an extra joyful of reunion. I joined Gina, who was sitting on the floor in front of the fresco and poured us each a glass of the bianca vino. She actually got rather giggly, quickly, as she drained her first glass of wine. She tried to apologize, saying that she must have over worked. She then made a crumpled face, realizing that it was time for lunch. Oh, I haven't eaten anything all day. You might have to help me to the lunchroom. She reached out and placed a loving hand on my cheek. "You are adorable, you know?"

I wasn't sure how to answer so I just smiled and enjoyed how my cheek was tingling at her touch. As I helped her up to a standing position, she leaned into me for support. She then put pretense aside and melted into my body, hugging me with both arms. I pushed aside a slight bit of Catarina guilt that tried to wedge between us and just enjoyed the spread of that wonderful warmness that was everything Gina. She smelled of fresh girly soap, hints of cinnamon and plaster—wonderful.

Lunch was Gnocchi alla Norcini, creamy with mushrooms and sausage, balanced with a variety of fresh garden greens—and some more wine. The spirit of the lunchroom was bright, as we enjoyed this classic potato pasta and relived stories of Todi and Marmore Falls. Gina, beautiful and joyful Gina, filled us in on what was becoming increasingly the consensus of our little once hidden fresco treasure. "As of today, I am rather certain that this fresco is even older than La Romita."

Chapter 24 Return to Terni

After our lunch, Gina went back to work and some of us went to work on our art. At this point, Gina had revealed a little more than half of the fresco. I took a break, made two espressos and brought them into her work cubby. She smiled and gladly slid her goggle eyewear off of her eyes and onto her head. I took a finger and caressed away some dust off her cheeks, which she also seemed to enjoy. We sipped our espressos, while I silently looked over what was revealed so far. My attention returned to Gina who was looking a little weary. "Why don't you take a break Gina? Let's escape for an hour or two?"

"I was just thinking the same thing Omar. Specifically, I want to show you some frescos right here in Terni."

With that, we headed down the hill, packed into her little smart car. She didn't have the luxury of a parking garage like Catarina had for her Ferrari, but she did have the convenience of her car's size. She parked 'Italian Style.' In other words, she fit into a space that was half street, half sidewalk. From there, it was a short walk to the church of San Francesco. We made our way along Via Carlo Goldini, which is one of those fun kind of Euro streets with an Island in the middle that holds café seating, colorful umbrellas and scooters. We made a quick stop at Risto Bar Cuccarini for a coffee to freshen our mental abilities. Ristobar Cuccarini is a cute *caffè* that offers a variety of sweet and savory, from its dramatic circular deli style refrigeration. Like so many cafes in Europe, it spills out on the street. We sat at their stylish counter seating, which has modern chairs at stool height, on the street, with the counter open to the interior. I suggested we return after our visit to the church for a glass of wine. Gina smiled, agreeing with a brightness in the eyes I was becoming progressively addicted to.

It was a bright day, which helped illuminate the cathedral. As we walked around in silence, I got the impression that Gina wanted me to make my own evaluations without her influencing my fresh eyes on the art that she had clearly studied before. Over coffee, she had let me know that I would be looking at the art of Bartolomeo di Tommaso, who lived in the early 1400's. There were quite a variety of scenes in the frescos of San Francesco—from scenes involving many figures to those, like several on columns, which pictured a single individual. Some of the frescos showed damage, but as a whole, they are in very good condition. I asked if she had worked on any of them and she confirmed that she had. This I found equally interesting, as well as intimidating, knowing that she had that kind of intimacy with this approximately 600 year old art. Imagine that, six hundred years. How many fathers of your father have been there since this very talented individual sweated over such amazing creations?

I suddenly had an epiphany. It was similar to the feeling I felt take me over when I was in Assisi. Looking at the work of Tommaso, it became clear to me the differences and similarities that I had been absorbing in all of the art that I had been studying. Though I had not seen this difference spoken about in the observations of the scholars of mid twentieth century Central Italy art, I finally felt an understanding that my small but highly curious brain could understand. Now, for the test. Could an expert like Gina appreciate my ideas? I certainly did not want to sound like an idiot to the woman that I was becoming so fond of.

"Gina, I have a thought to share."

"Yes, Omar."

"Tell me if I'm crazy, but ever since I've had my first epiphany in Assisi, I have felt something about the La Romita fresco. I should preface this with the uneducated observation that most of the frescos that I've been observing here in Umbria and through my Internet searches, have felt like they didn't have the same feel to me as what has been exposed at La Romita. Only since looking at Giotto's work in the upper Cathedral in Assisi and looking and Tommaso's art in front of us, have I felt a familiarity with our revealed fresco."

I was relieved that Gina's expression had not changed into one of amusement—she had not yet given me a look of you are cute but ridiculous. In fact, she actually looked interested and even encouraged me to continue. "Go on Omar."

"What is suddenly apparent to me Gina, is I'm no expert as you know, but when I've looked at the art of Signorelli and Fra Angelico in Orvieto, and both son and father Lippo in Spoleto, Perugino and most of the other art throughout Umbria, I felt something in common that I do not feel with Giotto and Tommaso."

"What is that Omar?"

"To me it is clear that Giotto, Tommaso and the artist of our mystery fresco, all preferred to paint the common man, the men and women of their reality. Oh sure they've had to dress them up religiously, both symbolically and also their landscapes. But I cannot get away from the feeling that I receive from their figures. That they are depicting real people dressed up to appease their religious and royal patrons. When I look at the art of most of the other painters of the mid-twentieth century, it feels as if their figures are regal, in other words, separated from the common man, elevated in some manner. I look at these figures in front of us and it almost feels like they are actors dressed up into a regal, religious situation. A situation that is not part of their real lives." I turned my attention back to the expert, expecting her to blow holes in my observations.

"Omar, my dear Omar, I think you are on to something here. I can add to your observations that many scholars have linked Tommaso to the Giotto School. In other words, it is very possible that Giotto and those who had studied with the master influenced him. Where as Giotto is thought of as the predecessor of the Renaissance, Tommaso and the Sienese School of which he is associated, are considered the precursors of the Umbrian Renaissance."

We made our way back to Risto Bar Cuccarini for the previously suggested glass of wine, where we continued our discussion of our fresco, Tommaso, and the art of his and Giotto's time. We also came up with a great plan to explore more of his art as well as to enjoy some more of Umbria's wine. I felt so comfortable with this woman. She felt like a tailored glove—a cozy pair that my hands longed to slip into. Well, maybe even more than my hands…

(see Tommaso Fresco Image in Appendix, page 252)

OMAR T in UMBRIA ITALY

Chapter 25 Foligno & Montefalco

The thoughts and revelations of the day before in the church of San Francisco, inspired a perfect follow-up day. Gina had proposed taking me to Foligno, the birth city of the artist Tommaso, which happens to be at the foot of the Montefalco wine region of Umbria. Thus, I suggested that we not only check out the Tommaso art in Foligno, but also visit the winery of Arnoldo Caprai. Both my father and Enrico wanted me to visit Montefalco and the Arnoldo Caprai winery in particular. It was suggested that as a relatively younger, "more modern," Umbrian winery, Arnoldo Caprai would offer some contrast to what I had seen thus far. It was also the winery that is responsible for developing the Sagrantino grape into something beyond its history as a dessert wine. Given my limited time in Umbria, I decided to include Enrico in our winery visit. Introducing the brother of Catarina to Gina was playing with fire, but I was feeling beyond worrying about such complications. Gina set up our ability to visit Tommaso's Foligno frescos, while Enrico arranged a tour and tasting at Arnoldo Caprai.

Fortunately, several works of Tommaso have survived in Foligno, his hometown. It was special being with Gina, not only because I was so attracted to her, she also had access to many places that were not readily available to the public. After a few calls we got to see all of Tommaso's work in Foligno. After a morning of inspection, Gina agreed with my concept that Tommaso, like Giotto, painted what felt like real people dressed up like actors in the painter's religious play. Keeping up with the Central Italian art scholar all morning was a challenge but fun. She pointed out many nuances in Tommaso's work that seemed at odds with our fresco—all very interesting. Most of all I just loved listening to her calm, bright mind as it worked. I, of course, also enjoyed just looking at her—such an unpretentious delight. Could we take things further? I was certain that the feelings were there. What I didn't know was if the fact that my stay was limited and other of life's complications would get in the way of what was clearly a wonderful connection.

A short drive from Foligno is the wine country of Montefalco, and we were soon at the Cantina Arnoldo Caprai. After a morning in Gina's territory, I was happy to return to ground more familiar to my hospitality history and me. The romance of a winery sitting among its vineyards is never lost on me, especially one that sits halfway up the gorgeous green slopes of the Umbrian hills. Above us, is the town of Montefalco, below a valley of lush patchwork of farms. Across the valley is another set of hillsides sharing their slopes with hilltowns such as Spello and Trevi—truly a gorgeous setting. Surrounding the winery, up and down, are the beauty and inspired hope of vineyards. The winery, which fit into the landscape beautifully, only adds to the surrounding beauty. Enrico was waiting for us. He had already met for a bit with some of the folks that he knew. They lent the lovely young Francesca to give Gina and me a quick tour while Enrico exchanged some wine with the powers to be. Francesca was lovely and informative. I also loved her classic Roman nose, which added character and strength to her delicate feminine features. When she would have some difficulty explaining things in English, she and Gina would confer and explain things to me together. They also shared some giggles, which I assumed were at my expense. Most interesting to me was the "test" vineyard of the prior mentioned Sagrantino grapes. The vineyard was set-up as collaboration with a nearby enology University program, to study and experiment with this grape. After centuries of use as only sweet wine, there was great excitement about its use into a potentially special, dry red wine. Enrico rejoined us with one of the wine maker assistants who was a friend. Along with the tasting room helper, Susana, they poured us some vintages of 100% Sagrantino wines that had been handled in a variety of ways—all part of the experimenting. Being such a high in tannins grape, it was a challenge for even my rather experienced palate to recognize the nuances, but boy was it fun to try. In a gesture that I thought rather romantic, Gina suggested they pour us only one glass of each wine. She stated that not being a connoisseur like the three of us that she would just prefer to share with me. I found her public announcement of her desire to share with me rather endearing. Enrico seemed to approve of my spending time with a woman other than his sister. I could tell that from the glint in his eye. More than that, Gina just had a manner that people enjoyed being around. In fact, it crossed my mind that Gina and Enrico shared similar honest, kind and intelligent dispositions. Two of the type that I call capital G—all good!

Gina had also kept her tasting under control so that she would be fine to drive us back to Terni and La Romita. I was feeling no pain; working very hard to attempt to distinguish the nuances of Sagrantino, taste after taste. No, I did very little spitting out. I just felt happy and relaxed, like I always seem to feel when I'm with Gina. Enough so that my hand would wander a little to one of her exposed shoulders and even her thigh a couple of times. I was not yet brave enough to allow my hand to linger; it just gave gentle pats and maybe even a little squeeze. All of my gestures received smiles and even a few pats and squeezes from her.

"So Omar, I happen to know that your group is going to Scheggiano tomorrow morning. I will be working on the fresco all morning, but how about I come meet you for lunch? There is a great restaurant that looks over the fish ponds."

"Ah my dear Gina, I can't imagine anything more delightful!"

"Wonderful, it is all set. I will be revealing an important piece of the fresco tomorrow. We will see if it still fits into your theory of it possibly being a work of Tommaso."

Chapter 26 Scheggiano

SCHEGGIONO
UMBRIA

We drove past Marmore falls, Casteldilago and Arrone. This is an incredibly beautiful valley, with its own river. Though the valley is mostly steep hillside, all of the rich flatland is filled to the max with stunning farmland. The hillsides are dotted with a plethora of quaint hilltowns.

I spent the morning in the old town with my ma. Scheggiano has wonderful nooks and crannies and is well maintained. We took a lot of photos and did some sketching. I then left Ma and the group; they headed back to La Romita for lunch. I made my way toward the restaurant where I would be meeting Gina. As you leave the old town, there is an incredibly scenic wide walking path lined that is with trees of both sides and a crystal clear stream. Conveniently, Gina pulled in just as I arrived.

On this warm day, Gina had on a simple frock, with sandal clad feet and an understated clip on one side of her hair. The clip looked old, antique. It held one side of her lovely long hair away from her face, while adding a touch of something extra. I asked and she confirmed that it was a hand me down from her Grandmother. In addition to admiring how she always looked so comfortable, I liked how the length of her frock did not cover much of her still youthful thighs. I did my best not to stare too long. I heard my sister's wisdom in my mind; warning my stray eyes to behave or she would smack me. Am I the only man who can never quite get away from a sister's always-present education on how to treat a woman with respect?

The pond, some 50 feet by 50 feet, was occupied by a dozen or so of ducks and swans, all surrounded with tall elegant trees. On both sides of us were steep green hills. Not many rays of sun are able to get through to this little paradise. Gina informed me that this used to be a fish farm. "Though it is no longer a commercial operation, as you will see, the fish still occupy the area. They still make their way upriver to spawn their young and make their way downriver to the source of food." She grabbed my hand and led me around the pool. Her hand felt so good, so comfortable. As comfortable as if it was my own hand, yet still skin bumper electric. With Gina's help, I too began to see the sleek, young trout fish going in and out of the camouflage of the bed plants. Gina had come prepared. Though I was sad when her hand left mine to pull out some goodies from her purse, I was delighted to see the excitement that she generated by throwing out her mix of seeds and grains to the ducks. Typical to this equally intelligent and conscience woman, she had abandoned the classic feeding of our feathered friends with bread. "It's like junk food to them," she informed me. Even the grandest white swan came over our way. Her size, white feathers and aloof movement, clearly separated her from the rest of the paddlers. My mind strayed long enough to Christian her as the Catarina of the feathered creatures that were swimming and cackling around us. I completely cracked up Gina when I began to quack back at them. Several of them seemed to enjoy that I spoke their language, albeit with what was certainly a different dialect.

Conveniently and romantically, overlooking the pond is restaurant Naiale. As we sat down to lunch, choosing the outdoor seating area, Gina filled me in on a little history. "Scheggiano is unusual in our old towns. Unlike most our historic villages, it sits on the lowland, next to the river." As she glanced at me for acknowledgement, I quickly raised my eyes from her exposed thighs and smiled at her. I must have had a somewhat childish look of guilt because she cracked up at my expression and my obvious manly indiscretion. After gathering herself, and apparently enjoying the fact that I had been staring at her thighs, she continued. "It may be so hard for us to imagine in this day where war seems far away from us in Umbrian, but there was a time where everything was about being somewhere protected."

This I understood from all of our hilltown visits. But instead of making a comment along those lines, I decided I liked her reaction to my wandering eyes and stated, "I am also greatly relieved that a beautiful woman like you feels that she doesn't have to overly protect those lovey thighs of yours…"

I said this so matter-of-factly, that it took her a moment to decipher and then respond with some more giggles and a little blush—after some wine, the blush stayed right on her cheeks and looked adorable. True, I had only formally met this woman a week ago, yet we had spent such quality time together. This, on top of how we met, how we were both drawn to each other like opposite poles of a magnet. Something was happening and it was happening fast. We ate, drank wine and talked away the rest of the afternoon. Where I found regular uncomfortable silences with Catarina, with Gina, everything seemed so natural and easy. In Catarina's defense, Gina was not burdened with an overloaded in debt family winery that she was compelled to try and sell me either. That being said, I just loved being in the presence of this girl. So much so, that my manly sexual drive even seemed tamed by her natural cheer. Despite how magical I found the before mentioned thighs, I was equally enamored with her eyes, hair and just how she moved. I could have just sat, watched and listened to her talk and I would have felt flush with joy. The delicious white wine and setting added to our mutual feeling of content. We did do a lot of touching, though I would call it very innocent, friendly. Despite my relaxed friendliness or perhaps because of it, Gina stopped and gave me that look. That look, that every man dreams to see on the face of a woman he has taken a fancy toward. Not sure if I was seeing what I thought I was seeing, I just stayed silent.

"Omar."

"Yes dear Gina."

"A…, do you have any plans for dinner?"

I locked onto her eyes for a while before I responded

"Nothing that cannot be changed instantly." In other words, as good as the food is at La Romita, I would certainly pass it up to be anywhere with Gina.

"How about for breakfast?"

When her cheeks got even redder than her natural wine infused pink, I was quite certain she was inviting me to stay the night with her. I pulled out my phone and texted my mother that I had received a very special invitation and that I would see her at La Romita after breakfast tomorrow. Before I sent it, I showed it to Gina who smiled and blushed again. My hand reached over to her shy chin. Gently I lifted her face back to mine and I kissed her. She responded in kind. These sparks of gentle kisses were wonderfully, dangerously kindling into fire. A fire that would be difficult to extinguish. When our lips finally broke we lingered on each others cheek for a while until I whispered, "What did you have in mind."

Off we went, in her tiny but sturdy smart car. This was actually my first time in these autos of the future. I had noticed on this trip through Rome, that they had started taking over that city. There are even single passenger versions now. You can't help but chuckle at the size and look of these babies that take up about the same space as a motorcycle. Like you, I'm sure, it was not lost on me the contrast of Gina's chariot, compared to Catarina's Ferrari. I admit to the fact that a sparkly thing easily gets the attention of Omar T, but I also can appreciate the practical and undemanding. I found Gina so lovely and pleasant to be around that I would be happy to be in an actual horse drawn chariot with her, even if a very competitive Charlton Heston was pursuing us. I also liked how close her smart car put me to her. Not to mention, with Catarina and the Ferrari, I had always felt nervous and tended to cling to the armrest in stressful fear.

VALLO DI NERA   Dreamer ARTB2, B2

Chapter 27 Vallo di Nera – Capulet and Montague

"Do you like cats Omar?"

Gina's offer started with a drive further up the valley, away from Terni. We followed the same river that Scheggiano lay near, past the small villages of Sant'Anatolia di Narco and Castel San Felice. We then left the floor of the valley and started to slowly climb up the rather steep hillside.

My answer to her question was, "I most certainly do, in fact, I often wish I were a cat."

This achieved the desired effect of gaining a chuckle out of my chauffer and now somewhat mysterious tour guide. "That's good, for we are about to enter the town of Vallo di Nera, which has two separate cat populations to go along with its all too few human residents. Sometimes we laugh about how the cats may outnumber us some day. We refer to them as the Capulets and the Montagues."

"You said 'we.' Do you live here?"

"Well, not exactly, because as you see, it is a rather a remote village." On cue, her little smart car, containing the two of us zipped around another turn as we slowly snaked up the hillside. "But I have an apartment here. Well, I still think of it as my grandparent's place; when they both passed away, I inherited it."

"Well I'm sorry to hear of your grandparents passing, but it must be nice to get away to a place like this for awhile."

She did not immediately respond, I wasn't sure if she was holding back some emotion or just concentrating on the winding road.

"It is a little more complicated than that Omar." She paused again for yet another turn involving a downshift and then two shifts up. "My parents died when I was young, so I came to live with my grandparents."

"So you grew up here?"

"Yes, though for high school, I left for boarding school in Terni and then on to University. Though I never moved back here, I would visit as often as possible. The 1997 earthquake, which is better known for the damage inflicted on the Basilica di San Francisco in Assisi, also badly damaged Vallo di Nera."

"Did you lose your grandparents in the quake?"

"Not exactly. My grandmother had just passed. My grandfather had a heart attack during the quake, which didn't kill him immediately but he didn't last much longer."

We were both silent for a while out of respect. I began to see the tops of some stone buildings as we approached the city. "The earthquake did do me some good. It was my motivation to get an additional degree at University and for me getting involved with the Institute. The city has been almost completely remodeled. As you will see, it is in great condition. That seemed somewhat an understatement. Vallo di Nera is so perfectly lovely that it gave me thoughts that this is the kind of place Disney would want to have created.

"First we visit the frescos of the Chiesa di Santa Maria Assunta and then we will do a little shopping. After that, we will walk up to the apartment."

I smiled at Gina. Her smile was equally welcoming. How very fortunate did I feel at that moment? I reached over, sliding my hand around her lovely feathered hair, on to her neck. I gave it a little appreciated squeeze, which was greeted with some reassuring pressure by her leaning her head onto my hand. Following our personal moment, she led me from the parking area to the church.

At this point, I had been in a lot of churches and I had stared at a lot of frescos. There was something about this peaceful church and its heavily patched frescos that I found very endearing, actually, moving. Somehow, the damage and patchwork gave an incredible sense of time and history. We walked mostly in silence. She pointed out some particular frescos and the history of any attempted restoration. I asked about the pockmarks in the wall of one section, wondering if they were what they looked like—they resembled machine gun fire. "No," responded Gina, "they are just a natural occurring blemish from the plaster aging." By the time we got to the alter, my emotions were getting the most of me. This time my hand landed on her shoulder. It then guided her into my embrace with our lips finding each other's. Ok, we didn't cause another earthquake, but I felt my foundation getting shaken—a spectacular spot for a kiss, and for a second, third and I don't know exactly how many. You could say we had difficulty stopping. Eventually we did make our way to the one and only town restaurant, which conveniently also functions as a *macellaio e venditore formaggio,* serving up many fine meats and cheese. We stocked up on both and some wine. We left our bags of goods behind the counter for a while. Gina announced that we must first take some offerings to the cats. We headed back past Santa Maria and down the hill where we did encounter a rather diverse looking group of cats. We stopped on the road above the lower road that they had made into a lair. Even before we started dropping goodies below, more furry critters appeared. Apparently, they sensed that Gina was bringing treats. We then headed for the high ground of Vallo di Nera. Here was another clowder of cats; these were mostly tabbies, resembling each other. It appeared that having the high ground seemed to encourage staying within ones demographic. They remained leery of me, but responded, as you would expect to a familiar provider.

Once back at the market, I insisted on carrying the goods as we climbed our way to her family apartment. It was small, as you would expect in this little postcard of a town. The views of the nearby Olive tree orchard, on its very steep slope, were wonderful. For the rest of the evening, I'm only going to let you use your own imagination. All I will say is that it was magical and that we interrupted each other's sleep more than once. Over a breakfast of croissants, an assortment of local cheeses and strong coffee, I asked the question that had come to mind on the afternoon before, when she had explained that they referred to their two separate cat populations as the Capulets and Montagues. "So dear Gina, have you had a Romeo Montague fall for a Juliet Capulet yet, and did it cause a big battle?" She laughed and leaned over and shared some slow wet kisses that I took as appreciation for my humor.

"Actually, we have noticed more and more changes in each group's coloring. Thus we believe there has been some romantic interludes."

With that additional comment, she returned to kissing. On our next break from kissing, I wondered out loud, "I'll bet the alpha elders are all in denial of the obvious romances…" This got another chuckle and some more sweet kisses.

Chapter 28 Narni

On this beautiful morning, our group was off to nearby Narni, which is not only a wonderfully laid out city, it has a few very interesting distinctions. First of all, I think of it as the portal to Umbria and everything that I love about this special part of Italy. Coming north from Rome on Highway E45, Narni is the first hilltown of Umbria to great you. The way it climbs its hillside is majestic, a suitable greeting for the province of hilltowns. You even get a glimpse of the Ponte di Augusto, an enormous arched remain from the grand Roman highway, Via Flaminia. They have also taken ownership of C.S. Lewis's Narnia, given the fact that the land of his imagination only adds an additional letter. Also, Narni is such an ancient, regal city, that the city's claim that they were in fact the inspiration for Lewis is very believable. As you enter the Narni museum, you are greeted by an ancient lion sculpture, their own Aslan, with "Narnia" celebrated above its remains. Narni, befitting its ancient history, is dotted with many churches. The grandest being right in its center, off its main, very busy piazza. Duomo San Giovenale and its 12th century origins, is not only grand, it also has a very fun crypt. Yes, fun and crypt seem like an oxymoron, but in a fantasy legend fitting for the inspiration for Narnia, there is a shrine, sacellum/crypt, housing a coffin with a big hole in the middle. Legend has it that whatever part of your body you stick in the hole, will receive its special healing powers. We all wondered if the hole would be big enough for our fellow student's whole head to fit in—she suffers from migraine headaches. If you have ever known anyone who suffers from these debilitating pains, you would understand the desire to try anything. We had fun with a group of us putting parts of our body into the hole and teasing each other. Fun!

Beyond the many things that make Narni special, I feel a strange but real personal connection to it. When I was much younger, I lost a dear friend. This friend and I used to call each other Nar, one of those silly nickname things that came from nothing, but grew to have special meaning. Thus, in addition to taking a lot of photographs for later sketches and finding good gelato, I had an additional mission for this day. It was to light a candle for her in the Duomo, near the healing hole. Once accomplished, I put my hand in the hole and then rubbed it on my chest, the best that I could do at getting my heart into the healing hole. I left the church with a smile on my face, feeling good about accomplishing my mission and that my Nar would also approve of Gina. As a man who mostly lives in the moment, this visit to the past actually ended with an even better feeling in the present.

My present was Gina and I was still floating on the incredible twenty-four hours we had spent together. This high gave pep to my step as I walked around Narni. Like the city of Spoleto, Narni is filled with little sanctuaries that you can make your own. Whether the formality of a *caffè* outdoor seating or a half hidden park with a view of a nearby hillside, Narni has a friendliness that seems to welcome everyone like you are a local or at least tied to its long history. I joined Jimmy and Sabrina, hanging with some locals outside the gelateria on piazza Garibaldi. I got a cappuccino and chose the combo of coconut and chocolate. Having me somewhat cornered, they demanded a summary of my day with Gina. As I danced around the adjectives of magical and special, they giggled and pressed for more details. Trying my best to keep the intimate details between Gina and me, I diverted the conversation to the relationship of the Capulet and Montague cats of Vallo di Nera. They gave up on getting more out of me and settled for a discussion of Shakespeare and how his words are still a part of a world so far removed from his time.

Back at La Romita, I was just finishing my lunch of Spaghetti with mushrooms, truffles and baby tomatoes, when Gina came rushing in and announced to all, you are not going to believe this… its all coming together….its

wonderful…its unbelievable!"

Chapter 29 A Deal

Before I explain what Gina discovered, there is more news I need to fill you in on. The night before my mother had received a call from my father. After their classic couple catch-up conversation, she handed the phone to me so that my father could inform me that he, Enrico, Catarina and the Senza Speranza board had reached a deal. He and his investors had purchased the winery with Enrico and Catarina. Brother and sister would be the new controlling partners with all of the board members being paid off. This was incredible news as I had so hoped that my amazing business father could work out a solution just like this. He also informed me how happy he was with my role in the process. He was pleased enough to let me know that the Omar T fun fund would be getting a nice influx of a cash bonus. This was exceptional news. Believing Catarina to be in Paris, I wondered how he had pulled off the deal, but decided not to go there. Sheepishly, I pondered if he might have any clue on some of the "handling" that I had had with Ms. Catarina. Knowing the discretion of my mother, I imagined that she would keep such info from my father— she liked to spare him of the details that he didn't need to know. As if reading my mind, when I glanced over she gave me a wink and a smile. I absorbed the wink and returned the smile.

As excited as I was with this news, I wouldn't be able to fill in Gina until after she shared what she was beaming over. She guided me to the studio and the fresco. I was shocked to see that the whole fresco had suddenly, magically seemed to be free of debris. She informed me that she was late arriving because she had needed a little sleep. "It all came together last night. I was so excited that I spent the whole night clearing the rest of the fresco. I didn't leave until five AM! I blew a kiss toward your room and then crashed for five hours. I've been cleaning it up some more for the last three hours. Do you recognize the scene Omar? You, being the man who compared the Tommaso and Giotto characters.

"It has looked familiar for a long time Gina but I haven't been able to place it…. Wait, I have seen this before, it is a copy of the Giotto scene from his cycle in the upper cathedral in Assisi – it's the scene of Saint Francis giving his cloak to a common man!"

But I was confused. "No, the cardinal is not Saint Francis and he is not giving a cloak to the man, he is taking it away from him, leaving him naked!"

I turned back to Gina who had such an expression of joy that these thoughts slipped my mind and just hung over us while I took her in my arms. When I finally broke our embrace I could see that she was crying.

She quickly appeased my worried face. "This is the most exciting thing that has ever happened to me as a restorer Omar. Even if the carbon-aging test does not confirm the most amazing possibility, I, we, are a part of something really special here. A story, an insight into history and the lives of people that were here, in this spot so very, very long ago."

She looked so weary. I pulled her back into another hug and just held her. At first I could feel some gentle sobs but she became rather strangely silent. Her body suddenly felt limp. I took me a minute to I realize that Gina had passed out.

SAN GEMINI
UMBRIA
ITALIA

Chapter 30 A Discovery

It turned out that Gina had been so wrapped up in the latest revelations that she had forgotten to eat dinner the night before and had slept right through breakfast time. Fortunately I got her to the lunchroom before our cooks, Franca and Egizia had left. They made her a plate of food, which I fed Gina one spoonful at a time.

My carrying an incoherent Gina from the studio, through the courtyard and into the lunchroom, attracted attention and some chatter. I was so busy looking after her that it took me a while to notice the crowd that had gathered and were watching us through the windows. Word apparently had gotten to Edmund, the director, who quickly joined us to see if there was anything he could do. It was about that time that Gina started to get some sense about her. A one point, she suddenly became aware that it was I who was holding and feeding her. She gave me a reassuring look of recognition, squeezed with both her now working hands and mumbled an "Omar, mm." before closing her eyes again and replacing her head on my shoulder.

As she leaned against me, I decided that I had better engage the very confused looking Edmund. I described how Gina was so excited about some discoveries that she had worked all night and finally passed out trying to fill me in. When Edmund asked what kind of discoveries, his words somehow brought Gina out of her trance. She looked up at Edmund and asked, "Are Ben and Valerio here?"

"Yes," answered Edmund.

"Can you get them?" She asked, seemingly finding some more strength as her consciousness grew and her excitement began to return. "It is important Edmund."

He nodded and went to collect the owner/architect and the La Romita assistant/historian as requested.

Soon, we had all three of the powers to be assembled for Gina to inform them of her findings. By the time they had joined us, she was sitting up, on her own, enjoying a mug of hot green tea.

A renewed Gina arose and led us to the studio. We helped her pull back the tarps, so that we could all view the now completely visible fresco. It was damaged with many bits and little pieces missing, but you could now make out the scene. "We now think that this is a replica of Giotto's famed Assisi scene with one important difference. In the original there is St. Francis giving away his cloak to the so-called "common man." Here we have a cardinal taking the cloak away, leaving the man naked. What we know for sure, is that whoever painted this, knew Giotto's fresco. What we will know tomorrow, when the results of the carbon dating arrive, is a better idea of when it was created. As I have discussed with all of you, from my experience, my feeling is that this wall is older than La Romita, that it was part of a structure that predated the 1576 date we have for the founding of the monastery."

Ben asked, "When did Giotto create the Assisi cycle?"

"The late 1200's until around 1304."

"So you are thinking our fresco was created some time between then and the founding of the monastery?"

"Yes I do, especially since you confirmed that it was already considered a possibility that this wall existed prior to the rest of the chapel, now art studio."

Edmund furthered the inquiry. "So, if it were painted before the monastery, that means it wasn't created by the La Romita monks. It could have been created by anyone?"

"*Corretto*, Edmund. Important to note however, that given its creation at that time of history, there were few known artists with this skill level."

I piped in. "What about Tommaso? Might this have been created by him?"

"Yes Omar, ever since our investigations of his frescos here in Terni and beyond, I have felt a stylish relationship with Tommaso and this fresco, but…"

"But you have your doubts?" This was from Valerio who was christened in the Terni Chiesa di San Francisco. The ceremony had taken place under the frescos of Tommaso.

"I probably shouldn't even suggest this until we have the carbon dating but ever since it was clear that this was a mock of the Giotto original, there was something very familiar that started to bother me."

"You mean beyond the fact that it was a copy of the Giotto?" I asked.

"That's right Omar. There was also something familiar about the cardinal taking the clothes off of this man."

Edmund spoke for all of us, "And have you figured it out?"

"I think so…, well…, at least part of it."

She looked at me so I asked, "What have you concluded Gina?"

"It was not so much figuring it out. It was correctly recalling something I read. First, I just had the feeling that I read something about an early renaissance painter that had to do with a disagreement with a cardinal – that some scholar had come into possession of a letter or a written document from that time that brought to life a disagreement between an artist and the Church. We have so little written from those times that its discovery was considered a really big deal."

Since I have been so in sync with this amazing lady these last few days, I suddenly saw where she was going with this. "Are you saying Gina that this fresco might have something to do with this dispute?"

"Yes Omar." She licked her lips as her eyes went back and forth between each of us. It was clear that she was a little uncomfortable with continuing. "Again this is premature until we get the dating information." She licked her lips again before continuing. "After finally remembering that the paper that I read was in fact the discovery of this document and that it was a dispute between the Church and an artist, it finally came to me where I had read this document."

She had all of our attention as she took a breath.

"The document discovery added a twist to the age-old argument of whether Giotto did in fact paint the cycle or whether it was actually done by someone else. This letter confirms that Giotto started the cycle, but leaves doubt that he finished them."

"And this means?" Edmund asked.

"As insane as this is going to sound to you all, I think that this fresco may have been painted by an angry Giotto after receiving this degrading document from the Church."

There may have been a plunk sound as all four of our chins immediately dropped in unison. We must have all looked so ridiculous that we actually turned Gina's serious expression into one that could not hold back from cracking up.

"I know that this sounds ridiculous and tomorrow's report will probably prove my theory impossible."

I think Ben, Edmund and Valerio were too shocked about the implications to speak. I, on the other hand, usually being slow at seeing what such things might mean for a place like La Romita, just smiled and took in the beauty standing before us.

Edmund finally gathered himself enough to ask, "You mean that you believe that we are standing in front of a fresco that was created some 800 years ago by the most famous painter of his time—the painter who was often credited with starting the renaissance some 200 years before anyone else was considered revolutionary enough to be regarded as going in the direction that he blazed?" Edmund's voice came out an octave or two higher than what we had all become accustomed to hearing from the rather relaxed director of the school. I noticed that Ben's cheeks had turned very red. He was apparently still unable to speak, but his eyes were flashing open and closed in quick succession. It occurred to me that perhaps he was calculating how such a possibility could change the economics of La Romita forever. Valerio just looked stumped, I wondered if he thought that Gina's words were too fantastic and that he probably felt that he was not accurate with translating them into his native Italian.

"There is more," offered Gina "Once I had completely exposed the hidden faces of the men, I realized that there was something familiar about their shape and expression. I pulled out my Giotto book and sure enough, I found both faces, though in different circumstances."

Gina reached to a chair, put both hands around a huge art book and opened it. First she showed us a painting of Giotto's in the lower chapel in Assisi, "Look at the face of this angel, its anguished expression." She held up the image next to the naked man in the fresco.

"Remarkable." This from the still red faced Ben.

Then I found our cardinal, though we know him as Judas, as Giotto depicted in Padua's The Kiss of Judas." She then held up the image of the Padua fresco and sure enough, our cardinal was the same man.

It turned out that we didn't have to wait until the next day. Just as I was thinking that Gina was the most amazing creature on the face of earth and each of the other three men present were going through their own deep thoughts, in walked one of Gina's co-workers from The Institute. He was carrying an opened manila envelope. He handed it to Gina with what I would call a cocky expression glowing on his face. She pulled out the contents, read it quickly, paused and then handed it to Valerio—probably since he was the only other native Italian present. He read the Italian words, smiled and handed it to Edmund. Typical to the always straight-faced, master teaser Edmund, his expression didn't change as he handed it to Ben.

I could not take it any longer and blurted out, "What the heck does it say?"

Gina turned to me and stated, "It says that the fresco plaster dates from the late twelve-hundreds."

Giotto: Angel in Anguish (Assisi)

Giotto: The Kiss of Judas (Padua)

Omar T's Sketch of the La Romita Fresco

Chapter 31 Perugia

The next morning we were off to the city of Perugia. This would be our last day trip. The ancient city of Perugia, where you can actually climb through history on an escalator. That's right, you can ride an escalator up to the old city. Along the way are some remains, dating back pre-Christ. Perugia first appears in written history as one of the 12 confederate cities of Etruria, 309-310BC. Even the time of Giotto, so fresh on all our minds, was young compared to the Etruscan period. Perugia is the capital of Umbria and its largest city, just under 200,000. We arrived on a Saturday, which is market day so not only did we have all of the amazing people watching of Corso Vannucci, we also had all of the goods and people interaction of the market. You come out of the escalator at one end of Corso Vannucci, right into the market, which is spread out in the piazza Italia. Corso Vannucci itself is filled with venders of its own, and street musicians. Many of the restaurants, *caffè*, and chocolatiers spill out onto the road with outdoor seating on this carless avenue—absolutely marvelous. Ma and I spent our last formal day of the school together. We enjoyed a brief skip through the market, down the Corso and into the majestic St. Lawrence's Cathedral at the opposite end of

Vannucci in the grand piazza di Quattro Novembre. Perugia is the furthest from La Romita of any of our drives this session. Thus, we were on our own for lunch before we would head back to La Romita in the late afternoon. As excited as I was to be around all of the discussion of the possible Giotto fresco, it turned out to be wonderful to have some time away to have some perspective.

Ma and I had grabbed a morning cappuccino at the Turan Café. It's strategic position turned out to be spectacular for people watching and sketching. It also had the bonus of the nicest bathroom of all of our travels in Umbria. Despite there being light traffic in this area, Café Turan has 5 or 6 outside tables that sit right against the street. We had so much fun that after our trip into the Cathedral, we returned for lunch, a second cappuccino and later some chocolate. It was a day that my mother and I will always cherish. I have never had more fun people watching. We canceled all of our plans for exploring more of Perugia and enjoying the finest Umbrian museum, the Galleria Nazionale dell'Umbria. First of all, you must understand that Perugia has a long history as a fashion and chocolate center—not a bad combo. Café Turan kept up the local tradition by making and stocking all kinds of chocolates. How fun to sample and just look at all of the goodies. We had so much fun comparing all of the women's fashions. The show was better than any catwalk. Ma and I had particular fun pointing out all the different and exciting designs of the women's shoes that passed by. Perugia is also a dog friendly town. Dog after dog pranced by, along with their various humans. How fun to compare them with their owners and vice versa. Directly across from us, were all the steps leading up to the Cathedral. This is a popular loiter zone. Not only because the oversized stone steps are a rather comfy place to sit and warm yourself under the bright fall sun, the view down Corso Vannucci is enticing in itself. Though the man in me is rather allergic to the concept of marriage, the romantic in me has got to love the ceremony of it all. It turned out that city hall is on the opposite side of the piazza from our vantage point. We watched wedding party after wedding party arrive and leave all hitched up. Not only did we have a variety of brides and wedding dresses to coo over, there were also some wonderful looking bride's maids and bride friends in some pretty hot dresses of their own—just looking, no tasting! One scene took place only about twenty-feet from our cappuccino table. The bride unloaded from a cab in what was perhaps the most spectacular wedding dress that I have ever seen. They had apparently already exchanged vows and came to the piazza just for its spectacular photo ops. I caught a photo of the groom and the best man, helping to re-fluff all of the bride's dress swirls, readying her for the photographer. Other wedding parties had special cars to photograph and take the bride and groom away. The entertainment was never ending.

Beyond all the high-end entertainment, there was also the occasional oddball that gave the scene an additional dimension—like the guy and the love of his life, his bicycle. As we watched all of the men and wives, this guy in his traditional logo dominated Italian biking wear, showed up. He went on to carry around his pride possession like it was a precious baby. He took photos of his bike against all the same gorgeous backdrops that the tourists and newly married couples were filling their cameras with. It was so surreal. Especially when he would contort his postures so that he could 'selfie' with the object of his obsession. Ma actually spit up a little cappuccino, when she started to laugh so uncontrollably at his antics and my comments of what I thought was going on in his tweaked mind.

In between all of the entertainment, Ma and I had a chance to review what was an incredible few weeks. In addition to the exciting fresco revelations, Father had successfully added a winery to his portfolio, keeping Enrico and Catarina as partners, which made me look good in their eyes too. As taken as I was with Gina, I also liked being thought of as special by a prince and princess of wine. My father was so pleased with how everything turned out that he was on a flight and would be signing papers the next day. His cheer was so good that he was bringing my sister along with him. We would all be celebrating the union with a party the next evening at Senza Speranza. All of the La Romita students and staff as well as the members of the Institute were invited to share the celebration with us.

Ben and Edmund were both excited and nervous about Gina's belief that La Romita now has a very special work of art. Gina found the article on the discovery of the alleged document from the church to Giotto by a local historian, Doctor Francesca Federico. Gina had already contacted Ms. Federico and the government agency in charge of Italy's historical preservation. Ma and I speculated that it was very fortunate that they were at the end of the La Romita season, which shuts down for the winter. This will allow all of the authorities time to go over the future of the fresco. Being Italy, I can imagine all kinds of spirited arguments to follow—both on Gina's theory and what to do about what appears to be a special piece of Italian history.

Gina promised to keep me in the loop. I imagine it will be stressful for her. She will probably have a lot of grenade like challenges come her way. As we enjoyed some more casual Perugia people watching, Mother coyly asked about a possible future for Gina and me.

"Well Ma, I told Gina that she can call me anytime, especially if she wants to share good news or she just needs someone to vent to. I suggested that when this revelation gets too crazy, as I'm sure it would, that she should get on a plane and come for a visit. I will personally guide her around all that is amazing on the Monterey Peninsula of California. I also mentioned that Dad would need someone to come check on the winery here and there and that I will make sure that he sends me."

This received a chuckle from my mother who then asked, "And what about Catarina?"

I added a nervous chuckle of my own. "Knowing Catarina, if I visit on a regular basis, I imagine there will be times where she will act like I'm her best friend and then other times where she treats me like the hired help."

"And maybe even jump your bones?"

"Mother, such language from my mother?" After a nice sampler of housemade chocolates, my mother had moved on to a glass of Campari and apparently was feeling no pain. She did however show a bit of a blush for her out of character remark, which made me join her in laughter. I added, "No doubt if it suits her, she will again attempt to seduce me, but I will, of course, fight her off."

This produced a wry smile and a stare down from my doubting mother.

"Well, most likely, since I am of the weaker gender, I will inevitably give in to her desires." We both cracked up at my confession. Changing away from the attention on Catarina, I added, "There will always be the reliable Enrico to keep the ship steady. He is a real treasure."

"So you say, I look forward to meeting Enrico tomorrow at the party." Added my mother. She then gave me a serious look.

She had apparently noticed the smallest of tweaks in my expression. "What is it Omar?"

"Well, Mother its just that I couldn't help noticing that when Gina and I joined Enrico at the Arnoldo Caprai winery, well… they… well they keep giving each other those kind of glances that communicate an attraction."

"Ah, I see, you think you might end up with some competition for Gina?"

"Yes, well…, no competition really. He is here and I'll be five thousand miles away."

"Hmm, how do you feel about that?"

"Frustrated, but they would be amazing together. They are both capital G's."

"Capital G?"

"All good!"

Chapter 32 A Party and a Celebration

Of course Catarina looked fabulous. She was wearing a dark blue sequined dress, wrapped tightly to her amazing figure, like the skin of an exotic lizard. She was unfazed with my arriving with Gina. She gave cheek kisses to Gina before giving me mine. Catarina then started to babble to Gina in Italian. As best I could follow, I think she was saying something along the lines of how Enrico had such wonderful things to say about her. Gina only got in a *grazie* or two in response before Catarina grabbed my mother, who also came with Gina and me. She guided mother away from us to the other side of the winery to introduce her to Enrico, who was sitting around a group of winery people, including my father.

I followed with Gina and introduced her to my father who was his usual suave self. He embraced her and told her how both his wife and his son thought she was super special.

La Romita bus driver, Raniero, brought all of the other students and the La Romita staff. There was such a joy in the air. Another successful La Romita season was finishing. That in itself was worthy of a party. And of course there was a lot of excitement over the fresco, as well as the wonder of what the future will unveil. There were also the dual emotions of soon leaving this paradise for the comfort of home. Alice from Florida expressed this well, "I'm so sad to leave, but I can't wait to see my horses!" La Romita cooks Egesia and Franca were delighted to get the night off from cooking and joined the party. I talked food with Egesia in a mix of Italian and English—food is a rather universal language. Since, Franca enunciates one of the most beautiful "grazie" my ears have ever enjoyed, I am always saying thank you to her in hopes of hearing her magical version. I solicited a couple more on this grand evening. All the members of our class were jubilant with this chance to finish our special time together. The wine was flowing.

I passed by Edmund and Enrico who were planning ahead. They were discussing how Senza Speranza should be a future regular stop for the students of La Romita. Ma, not being the jealous type, seemed to enjoy my father dancing with Catarina as much as he did. I watched Jimmy guide Sabrina away from a group of shy winery workers. She was once again working her magic of somehow connecting with those who did not even share a common language.

Edmund and Valerio brought along their band, which added some jazzy tones to the happy crowd. We were all gathered among the wine barrels, which doubled nicely as a place for a party. The tall Jimmy and the short Sabrina were unfazed by the awkwardness of their attempting to dance together— it just fueled their insatiable laughter. Jimmy swung Sabrina into my arms so that I could swing her around a little myself. This gave me a chance to thank her personally for adding so much life to our group and to wish her luck in her two week additional stay in the town of Orvieto—her grandiose smile beamed with anticipation. I joined the group of Gina, Valerio and Dr. Francesca Federico, who were discussing the fresco. They were all so excited with the possibilities that I didn't need to understand their Italian. I just smiled and soaked in their enthusiasm.

"Imagine, a fresco, possibly by Giotto was staring at me all of the time that I was reshaping La Romita." This was from Ben, the architect/owner. "There is something reassuring but also spooky about the whole thing." With this, I had to agree…

My sister, being my sister, finally appeared. She is her own woman, very independent. She had been off with Enrico's assistant winemaker, Anna. You must understand that my sister is a kind of a genius when it comes to language. After studying in Europe following high school, she came back speaking French, Italian and Spanish, also pretty good German, Czech, and Portuguese.

I guided her to the dance floor. We did little but slide a foot here and there as we were so busy catching up. You see, my sister is often a kind of the right hand man in my adventurous life. We seem to especially value each other since our significant others have a habit of going, soon after coming. Via email, I had kept her up to speed to some degree on our going ons in Umbria, but there was plenty to quiz me about. Sissy, being Sissy, was mostly teasing me about Catarina and inquiring about Gina. My sister is an interesting mix of being somewhat shy as well as sometimes fearless. I think she also lives a bit vicariously through all of my encounters. Can you be shy and fearless? Well, that is how my sister sounded when she spoke of Enrico and his assistant Anna. I got the impression that she might fight me for being Father's future liaison to Senza Speranza. I nervously noticed Enrico was dancing with Gina—*che fai*—what ya goina do?

Catarina, being Catarina, came between Sissy and me. Before stealing me from my sister, she complemented Sissy on how intelligent she was and how she had so enjoyed spending the day with her and my father.

"Oh Omar, what am I to do with you?" Asked Catarina as we rather effortlessly made our way around the dance floor.

"Catarina, oh *bella* Catarina, what am I to do with you?"

This did get her to laugh, which gave me time to give her a spin before bringing close those deep, rich brown eyes.

"Catarina, you know as well as me that you will do whatever you want with whomever you want, when you want."

This brought some more chuckles before she confirmed. "*Si, certo*!" She then smiled before adding, "But I will not keep you from Gina… I do approve by the way."

With her approval dancing in the air, not knowing where to land, she gave me a little spin and walked off with her typical commanding authority.

As per usual, the departing sway of her bottom was grabbing my attention. Seeing my stare and knowing how badly such might appear to Gina, my sister always looking after me, abruptly grabbed my attention away from Catarina. She then appropriately led me over to Gina. The two of them hit it off immediately. Soon they left me behind by switching to Italian. This did give me a chance to survey the room and take in all the joy and adventure represented before my eyes. *Che bello!*

Omar T in Umbrian Glossary

Fiction & Reality
Somewhat Alphabetical (R)=Real (F)=Fiction

*There is in fact a wall in the La Romita chapel/studio that is believed to possibly be even older than the sixteenth century structure. There is no reason to believe there is a hidden fresco within its ancient stone and plaster, but…

Bartolomeo di Tommaso (R) The art of this fifteenth century painter is an Umbrian treasure waiting to be more discovered.

Emma Shapplin (R) Perhaps the greatest voice per pound that I have ever encountered. You can enjoy the full range of this voice in classic opera or her creative pop/rock. Whenever I hear her voice or think of her beauty, I feel better about everything.

Dr. Francesca Federico (R) Though her mention in the book is a fictional account, she is a real Umbrian historian and friend of Valerio, who helped me with some historical detail.

Giotto (R) One could argue that all of the iconic Italian art that we love so much, all came from this thirteenth century painter.

International Institute for Restoration and Preservation Studies (F&R) The Institute mention and the character of Gina are fictional accounts. However there is a real study abroad program. http://www.sangeministudies.org

Iris Litt (R) Exceptionally gorgeous glass art.
http://www.irisglassdesign.com

La Romita Staff (R) All those mentioned in the book are real and as of 2016, were members of the staff. Special thanks to Edmund and Valerio for helping me to add some polish to this novel. Add to your Umbrian collection by picking up a copy of Edmund's beautiful poetry.

La Romita Students (R) All of the La Romita students mentioned in this book are real, though their accounts in this story are fictional. My mother and I had wonderfully inspiring groups in both 2010 and 2016.

Senza Speranza (F) Translating to "without a hope," my naming of this fictional winery was a kind of ode to all my friends who are brave enough to be a part of the romantic but rarely, very profitable wine business.

Wineries of Umbria (R) The other two wineries mentioned, Lungaretti and Arnaldo Caprai are both real as are the wine regions of Torgiano and Montefalco and are as wonderful as I describe.

Umbrian Restaurants, cafes, bars (R) All those mentioned in the book are real. The mentioned Misha of Mishima is actually a Michelle. The book chapters are for the most part organized by Umbrian towns. Thus travelers can easily refer to Omar's experiences while visiting each place themselves!

And:

Pajaro Street Grill (R) A dinner only restaurant, two blocks from Oldtown, Main Street, Salinas, opened by the author in 1999 - birthplace of Omar T Black and a home of Central Coast Cuisine, Belly Dance Fundraisers, Wine Club and exceptional conversation.

Royce's restaurant, Monterey CA (F) fictional but has resemblance to the author's restaurant, Pajaro Street Grill in Salinas CA – named after a great Utah restaurateur, Royce Rosendaal. Royce was responsible for the author's first restaurant job.

Giotto Assisi controversy
Follow-up articles for those wanting more info:

http://www.telegraph.co.uk/news/worldnews/europe/italy/9658520/Assisi-fresco-restoration-proves-it-was-Giotto.html

https://news.artnet.com/art-world/appalling-restoration-destroys-giotto-frescoes-at-the-basilica-of-saint-francis-in-assisi-261811
https://www.theguardian.com/artanddesign/2015/feb/19/italian-art-medieval-frescoes-damage
http://www.reuters.com/article/us-art-italy-giotto-idUSBRE8B514020121206

http://www.wga.hu/tours/giotto/assisi/index111.html

http://www.nytimes.com/2001/07/28/arts/under-a-shroud-of-kitsch-may-lie-a-master-s-art.html

Bartolomeo di Tommaso (Terni – Chiesa di San Francisco) (R)

Omar's Umbrian Recipes:
Recipe Glossary

Tbl = tablespoon
t = teaspoon
lbs = pound
oz = ounce

Note: Salt, for Omar T is either Kosher or Sea Salt
*throw away your highly refined salts
These are Omar's recipes, many similar dishes are served at
La Romita. For actual La Romita recipes, get **Palates &
Palettes**, La Romita's Cookbook

https://www.createspace.com/4395408
or
https://www.amazon.com/Palates-Palettes-Cookbook-Alessandro-
Quargnali-Linsley/dp/0989828808/

Crostini and Bruschetta

A staple of Mediterranean cooking, Italy in particular, are
crostini and bruschetta. Slice up your leftover bread and
baste it with garlic oil and bake around 10 minutes and you
have your base for any toppings. I keep whole garlic in
olive oil with a sprig of rosemary so that I can add this
touch of Italy anytime. For instant garlic oil, mince your
garlic before adding it to your olive oil. The classic
bruschetta topping is homegrown chopped tomatoes,
minced garlic and chopped basil, all tossed with some salt
and olive oil. Have fun making up your own bruschetta with
chopped and minced goodies that you are fond of. A soft
cheese, like a goat cheese, spread on your crostini, makes a
great base for adding pesto or tapenade. ENJOY!

Fried Squash Blossoms

3/4 cup cornstarch
1 t baking powder
1/4 t pepper
1/4 cup flour
1/2 t season salt

1/2 cup water
1 egg -- slightly beaten

10 to 15 squash blossoms
1/2 cup whole-milk ricotta
1/4 cup mayonnaise
1 t dried oregano
1 Tbl bread crumbs
Vegetable oil
Salt & Pepper to taste

First, make the batter. Combine the first 5 ingredients, and then stir in the egg and water until smooth. Store in the refrigerator for 15 to 20 minutes.

While the batter is chilling, prepare the squash blossoms. Carefully separate the flower petals without breaking them and remove the pistil in the center. Combine the cheese, mayonnaise, oregano, and breadcrumbs until smooth. Carefully add about a tablespoon of this mixture to each blossom and twist the top of the flower tight.

Heat enough oil in a frying pan - about an inch deep - to accommodate the blossoms. Get the batter out of the fridge and dip each blossom in batter, coating it. Carefully place each batter-covered blossom in the hot oil and fry until golden crisp on both sides. Remove and drain on paper towels, then sprinkle with salt and pepper. Enjoy!

Tartufo (Truffle) Risotto

One secret to a good risotto or creamy polenta, is to add your fats a little at a time and work it, work it. Ideally, use a heavy (strong) whisk to work the risotto. Imagine you are an Italian Grandmother with strong forearms and resolve ☺

4 Tbl (1/2 stick) butter, divided in ½ inch cubes
1 large onion, chopped
1 t minced garlic
1 Tbl extra-virgin olive oil
1 1/4 cups Arborio rice or medium-grain white rice
1/2 cup dry white wine.
4 cups (quart) chicken or vegetable broth.
2 t shaved or chopped black truffle
Optional: truffle oil
1/2 cup grated Parmesan cheese
Chopped fresh parsley

In a saucepan big enough to handle the risotto's expansion, start by sautéing 1 large onion in a TBL extra-virgin olive oil. Add 1 ¼ cups Arborio rice. Stir the rice in the sautéing onions for five minutes. Then add ½ cup dry white wine and the garlic. Simmer till liquid reduces one half. Add the butter, stirring as it melts. Add a ½ cup of stock while stirring with whisk. Continue the introduction of stock ½ cup at a time, working the rice with your whisk. Add the truffles. Taste the rice – add salt, pepper, truffle oil to your taste. Finish with the Parmesan cheese and chopped parsley.

<u>Spaghetti Carbonara</u>

1 pound dry spaghetti
2 Tbl extra-virgin olive oil
4 oz pancetta or bacon, sliced into thin strips
4 garlic cloves, minced
2 egg yolks
1 cup freshly grated Parmigiano-Reggiano,
Freshly ground black pepper
1 handful fresh flat-leaf parsley, chopped

Bring a large pot of salted water to a boil, add the pasta and
cook for 8 to 10 minutes or until tender yet firm "al dente"
Heat the olive oil in a deep skillet over medium flame. Add
the pancetta and sauté for about 3 minutes, until the bacon is
crisp and the fat is rendered. Toss the garlic into the fat and
sauté for less than 1 minute to soften.

Add the hot, drained spaghetti to the pan and toss for 2
minutes to coat the strands in the bacon fat

Finish:
Turn off the heat – add the egg yolks and toss with the
noodles, then add the cheese and toss. Plate the Carbonara
with the addition of some more grated cheese and the
parsley on top.
For those with flare: Bring your saucepan and its contents to
the table. Perform the final steps with the egg and cheese in
front of your guests, Omar style!!!

<u>Osso Buco</u>

2 – 3 lbs cut veal shanks
1/4 cup flour
1/4 cup olive oil
2 cloves garlic, minced
Mirepoix:
Chopped 1 large onion, 1 large carrot, 1 Celery stick
1 cup dry white wine
1 cup chicken or beef stock
32 oz diced tomatoes
1 dry bay leaf (do you love rosemary, thyme? Add them too)
salt and pepper to taste
Gremolata: 1/2 cup chopped fresh flat leaf parsley 1 clove
garlic, 2 t grated lemon zest – food process or hand mince
into a pesto.

Dust the veal shanks lightly with flour. Sweat/sauté the
Mirepoix veggies in a large skillet over medium to medium-
high heat in the olive oil. Add the shanks, and cook until
browned on the outside of both sides. Remove to a bowl.
Add the garlic, bay leaf and any other chopped herbs, to the
skillet; cook and stir until tender. Return the veal to the pan
and mix in the wine. Simmer for 10 minutes.
Pour in the tomatoes and chicken/beef stock, and season
with salt and pepper lightly. Cover, and simmer over low
heat for 1 1/2 hours or place in oven (350 °) basting the veal
every 15 minutes or so. The meat should be tender, but not
too easily falling off of the bone.

Sprinkle the Gremolata over the veal just before serving.
Traditionally, serve with a cocktail fork for scooping out the
treasure that is the bone marrow.

Gnocchi alla Norcini

Gnocchi
3 Medium to Large Potatoes (About 2 1/2 lbs)
1 1/2 Cups All-purpose Flour (and Extra For Rolling)
1/2 t Salt
2 Egg Yolks

Bake or steam Yukon Gold or Russett Potatoes (I microwave between two plates in a little water) Separate from skins and mash Add the egg yolks, and slowly start adding the flour a little at a time, mixing gently with your hands and continue until you have created a soft workable dough. Knead gently until you have achieved a smooth, pliable if slightly sticky dough.
To shape the gnocchi, first break the dough into fist-sized pieces, and roll each piece into a log about the thickness of your thumb on a lightly floured surface.
Cut into 1 inch pieces. Place the prepared gnocchi on a lightly floured baking sheet and keep refrigerated until ready to use.

SAUCE:
4 Italian sausages chopped
8 oz fresh mushrooms, cleaned and coarsely chopped
1/2 cup chopped onion
2 cloves garlic, peeled & minced
2 Tbl olive oil
1 cup dry white wine
Salt & Pepper
red pepper flakes (optional)
1 1/2 cups heavy cream

In a heavy saucepan sweat/sauté the onions with a pinch of salt and pepper in the oil, adding the sausage—stir and brown. Add the garlic and mushrooms. Stir briefly and then add the wine. If you want to spice it up add some red pepper flakes here. Reduce the liquid by half.

Add the cream and check your seasoning and adjust to taste with salt, red pepper flakes and black pepper.

Continue to cook over medium low heat until the sauce has thickened, about 10 minutes. If you are using, milk, ½ and ½ or a substitute such as almond milk or soy, add some grated cheese to help thicken the sauce.

FINISH:

Once you have your sauce, cook your gnocchi:
drop carefully into salted boiling water and remove when they float to the surface.

Drain, return to the pot and add half the sauce.

Gently toss the gnocchi to coat with the sauce, then spoon the gnocchi into individual bowls.

Serve the gnocchi, with an extra scoop of sauce on top.

Finish with grated Pecorino Romano cheese

Omar T Anecdotes

How Omar missed the Assisi Cathedral (Chapter 11 reference)

Before my first visit to Umbria and La Romita with my
mother, I decided it best to work on my dulled painting
talents in an attempt to sharpen them up. I dug through my
mother's deep drawers of Umbrian Images. I found one of a
group of folks, wonderfully spread out on the steps of a
classic hilltown, steep and narrow walkway. The image was
in her Assisi file. I asked her if she remembered taking the
picture. She did not, nor could she identify where in Assisi
she had taken the photograph. It was a perfect image to
remind me how to paint in Italy. It had the starkness of the
aged architecture and the color of people intertwining
themselves with the landscape. Though the painting itself
did not turn out well as I worked it, and overworked it, it
was an excellent tool in exciting me for our upcoming
workshop. It also gave me a quest. I was determined to find
the spot in Assisi that I had been working on for such an
extended amount of time. Once in Assisi, I decided to
approach this quest in a systematic manner. I would start
from the opposite end, away from the Grand Cathedral,
Basilica Saint Francis, gradually making my way toward it.
In typical Omar T fashion, I was constantly diverted from
my goal by the next shiny thing. There were so many
interesting people and scenes that kept interrupting my
quest. My early treads were away from the typical tourist
routes so I tended to discover the aspects of Assisi, which
were interesting in a hilltown culture kind of way—very
endearing. The biggest diversion came at the high point of
Assisi. Here lies the Rocca Maggiore, Medieval fortress, as
well as some incredible views of the numerous church
spires and towers of town, the farmland below and the lush
hillsides on the other side of the mountain. From this
viewpoint, I ended up on a path that skirts the city on its

topside—a very peaceful path through lush green shrubbery. The upper side of this mysterious path is framed by a stone wall that feels like it has been there forever. The underside of the walkway is sometimes so lush that you feel lost in nature, then suddenly there is enough of a break to see through to some backyards, the city below and the patchwork of farmland in the valley—all breath taking with the added feeling that so few ever discover and walk this path within *the so tread upon* Assisi. After emerging from this walk in the heavens, I was in a kind of bliss. I was much less concerned with finding the location of my quest. Nonetheless, I continued looking and though I still did not find the object of my search, I came upon several less visited churches and other interesting scenes. At this point I knew that my time must be running short so I consulted my mini Assisi map created by the La Romita Director, Edmund. With its help, I headed toward the main square. As I emerged from a side street at about a mid-point in a long, steep pathway, I felt a familiarity. It was familiar but confusing. I had only viewed this pathway from my mother's photograph, which was the view of looking up from below, not standing in the middle of it. More and more aspects looked familiar but I was still uncertain until I reached the bottom of the stairs and looked-up. Sure enough, I had found the object of my quest. Ironically, it was right off of the main piazza. If I would have walked the normal tourist path of Assisi, I would have discovered it within a half hour of entering the town. I took some photos of my own and felt a kind of ironic spiritual discovery within this town of religious migration. As I rushed to make the bus for our return, I only had time to look at the Basilica as I walked by. Though I was sad at not getting in to visit its treasures, I vowed to return. I chuckled an Omar T type of laugh to myself about my little adventure within an adventure…

La Romita School of Art, Terni Italy

http://www.laromita.org

La Romita Cookbook: **Palates & Palettes**
https://www.createspace.com/4395408

Edmund Zimmerman's Book of Poetry: Division Symbol
http://www.edizionithyrus.it

Continue the adventures with Omar T:
OMAR T in MONTEREY

Omar's Monterey adventures are fed by the literature of John Steinbeck, the eccentricities of Salvador Dali and the amazing beauty and foodstuffs of California's Central Coast.

OMAR T in SAN DIEGO & TIJUANA

Omar's San Diego and Tijuana adventures are fed by the insights of Dr. Seuss, the regions craft beer and food culture as well as the unique history of these two border cities.

OMAR T in SAN FRANCISCO

Omar and his sister adventure to nearby San Francisco to help create a new restaurant. Their successful Monterey restaurateur of a father has entered in a partnership with a SF businessman who's youth was colored by the alternative culture lived and written about by the great Beat writers such as Kerouac, Burroughs and Ginsburg. In this book, Omar, not only has to try and understand the Beat counter culture history, he has to deal with his own ghost from the past. Fortunately, he not only has the support of his "Sissy," he is also helped by a mysterious Bodhisattva.

*Each Omar Story is independent; they do not have to be read in order, though there are some treats for those who do.

Coming Soon: **OMAR T in NEW YORK**

The Beat writers and Omar continue a relationship as Omar moves to the Big Apple to help with the opening of a new restaurant in the Iconic Chelsea Hotel.

OMAR T in SALT LAKE CITY

Omar finds himself in the middle of a kidnapping as well as some interesting Mormon history and of course some great food.

And then: OMAR is off to PARIS, NEW ORLEANS, HONG KONG, SINGAPORE LAS VEGAS, ISTANBUL AND AFRICA And then …

Also Coming Soon:

UMBILICAL CORD with co-author/humanitarian

Tererai Trent

*Named by Oprah Winfrey as her favorite all-time Guest!
A collection of African short stories

DEAMER'S AMAZON AUTHOR PAGE
https://www.amazon.com/author/deamerdunn

Additional novels by Deamer:

STRENGTH AND GRACE

Strength and Grace is the story of a young Mexican woman who stumbles into becoming a bullfighter. She so excels that she becomes a great Matador. The catch is that all but a few think that she is a man. It is a story of female empowerment within the Mexican male culture of the bullfight. There are also coming of age aspects to the story as the reader follows her growth from being a fifteen-year old tomboy to a twenty-five year old woman who spends the majority of her time being a man. This duality creates gender identity issues that she must face along with all of the dangers of her profession and the tension of her masquerade.

Winner, one of the best fiction novels of 2015, Southern California Book Festival
Winner, one of the best fiction novels of 2015, Great Midwest Book Festival

Also available in Español
FUERZA y GRACIA

MEETANDTELL.COM/ADVENTURE

Winner, one of best romance novels of 2016
Los Angeles Book Festival

What is more adventurous than looking for and starting a romantic relationship? Especially with all of the new tools and avenues that the Internet has brought to the tips of our fingers. Clark and Ronda's generation began to date before there was a World Wide Web. As they are drawn inside this new magical world, they bring the perspective of experiencing dating before and after the Internet. Two friends in their forties, Clark and Ronda, take us along on their adventure to meet, start and incorporate relationships into their already mature lives. Clark alternates with Ronda in telling their first person accounts. The story opens with Ronda as a veteran online dater, while Clark reluctantly joins a practice that he sees as belonging to younger generations. What starts as casual fun soon develops into more serious adventure, romance, disappointment and even danger. In a reflection of our time of quick messages, tweets and texts, the chapters are short. They bounce back and forth from the male and female perspectives of Clark and Ronda. This is a story of two people, who are in the timeless pursuit of love, during a time of fascinating changes.

Deamer Sketchbooks:

In case you haven't heard, coloring books for adults are becoming quite a passion. For many, perhaps a little coloring can still feed a need for getting into a book and more easily allow the satisfaction of finishing something. Why settle for a computer created book when you can add life to original sketches? Each sketch is accompanied with a blank page for you to add comments and notes for your life or your own artistic doodles. The idea is that this is a book that you can make your own. Each Deamer Sketchbook also includes some original short stories.

Additional Books from
PAJARO STREET PUBLISHING:

RM Blake EROTICA:
EROTIC REFLECTIONS

This book of erotica includes twenty-two stories, eleven told by a woman, eleven recalled by a man. Though mostly heterosexual tales, there are a few stories that blur such distinct lines. This collection has a diversity of ages, marital status and circumstances. Rather than filling these pages with a lot of lustful adjectives, there is an attempt at concentrating more on sexual frankness, colored with humor. The goal is to feed the voyeur, inspire sexual creativity as well as build health, honesty and respect in your sexual relations.

RM BLAKE EROTICA COMING SOON:
THE SEXUAL EDUCATION OF ZOE
AND
THE SEXUAL EDUCATION OF COLIN

These two companion novels mirror each other. Young Zoe approaches her favorite professor to help her further her education. She successfully persuades the doctor of creative writing to take her understanding of sex and human relations to a whole different level.

Colin, like Zoe is also from a difficult background. In this book, his much older professor of philosophy approaches her promising student with continuing his education in her bedroom. Both professors have strict rules and a timetable for their student's sexual education.

Readers are invited along for this extra curricular education that goes not only into the details of sex and human anatomy, the openness and timing of these relations invites all four to deal with their past history and emotions going forward.

Also Coming from the author RM Blake:

Love Song Journals

Poignant stories of loss and love

Love Song Journals: **Stephen and Linda**
So many of us face addiction, obsession and a drive of compulsion. These drives can create beauty as well as destroy. Linda, shackled with addiction, found her great love in Stephen a good-hearted man of individual drive. Their compulsion for each of other would bring great adventure to their love, while their drives in life would also demand times of separation. This is the story of a twenty-two year romance through life and death. It is colored by the fury creatures of Jasper and Muffy that became integral parts of this couple's lives.

Love Song Journals: **Joseph and Mickey**
Love later in life can often be complicated. Relationships and history between each lover's families can put a strain on love. The story of Joseph and Mickey is one of the beauty of finding someone with differences that actually balance and enhance each other's life. This is also a tale of the tragedy of something beyond the control of lovers getting between them. Sometimes the combining of friends and family are just not compatible.

About RM Blake

RM Blake is a pen name, which keeps the author's identity, age, race, gender and sexual preferences private. RM is a collective voice of love, passion, empathy, and understanding. The author wishes each reader to approach the author's literature with an equally open mind. That being said, RM would love to hear from you.
rmblake@artbz.bz

About the Author

Deamer was born and raised in Salt Lake City, Utah. He lived in Switzerland and the Washington D.C. area before settling in Monterey County California in the early 1980's. He currently resides in the birth city of John Steinbeck, Salinas California, the former home of his dinner only restaurant, Pajaro Street Grill. Deamer now spends much of his time in Tijuana Mexico and traveling the world with his recurring character, Omar T Black. "I have a list of some thirty more locations I hope to write Omar adventures– come join the journey!

http://artbz.bz

"Everyday is a great day to read a book or color one!!!"

Keep in touch with Deamer, as Omar travels the world, deamer@artbz.bz! Please pass on your impressions; write a review on Amazon and/or other sites such as Goodreads – your thoughts can really make a difference! Most your local bookstores can also get you Deamer novels at the same price as Amazon ☺

https://www.amazon.com/author/deamerdunn

Made in the USA
Lexington, KY
27 October 2019

56112776R00165